THE SUNSET LIMITED

A NOVEL IN DRAMATIC FORM
BY **CORMAC McCARTHY**

★

★

DRAMATISTS
PLAY SERVICE
INC.

THE SUNSET LIMITED
Copyright © 2006, M-71, Ltd.

THE SUNSET LIMITED received its world premiere by Steppenwolf Theatre Company (Martha Lavey, Artistic Director; David Hawkanson, Executive Director) in Chicago, Illinois, in May 2006. It was directed by Sheldon Patinkin; the set design was by Scott Neale; the costume design was by Tatjana Radisic; the lighting design was by Keith Parham; the sound design was by Martha Wegener; the casting was by Erica Daniels; and the dramaturgy was by Ed Sobel. The cast was as follows:

BLACK .... Freeman Coffey
WHITE .... Austin Pendleton

The Steppenwolf production of THE SUNSET LIMITED subsequently premiered in New York City in October 2006.

CHARACTERS

BLACK

WHITE

THE SUNSET LIMITED

This is a room in a tenement building in a black ghetto in New York City. There is a kitchen with a stove and a large refrigerator. A door to the outer hallway and another presumably to a bedroom. The hallway door is fitted with a bizarre collection of locks and bars. There is a cheap formica table in the room and two chrome and plastic chairs. There is a drawer in the table. On the table is a Bible and a newspaper. A pair of glasses. A pad and pencil. A large black man is sitting in one chair (stage right) and in the other a middle-aged white man dressed in running pants and athletic shoes. He wears a T-shirt and the jacket — which matches the pants — hangs on the chair behind him.

BLACK. So what am I supposed to do with you, Professor?

WHITE. Why are you supposed to do anything?

BLACK. I done told you. This aint none of my doin. I left out of here this mornin to go to work you wasnt no part of my plans at all. But here you is.

WHITE. It doesnt mean anything. Everything that happens doesnt mean something else.

BLACK. Mm hm. It dont.

WHITE. No. It doesnt.

BLACK. What's it mean then?

WHITE. It doesnt mean anything. You run into people and maybe some of them are in trouble or whatever but it doesnt mean that you're responsible for them.

BLACK. Mm hm.

WHITE. Anyway, people who are always looking out for perfect strangers are very often people who wont look out for the ones they're supposed to look out for. In my opinion. If you're just doing what you're supposed to then you dont get to be a hero.

BLACK. And that would be me.

WHITE. I dont know. Would it?

BLACK. Well, I can see how they might be some truth in that. But in this particular case I might say I sure didnt know what sort of person I was supposed to be on the lookout for or what I was supposed to do when I found him. In this particular case they wasnt but one thing to go by.

WHITE. And that was?

BLACK. That was that there he is standin there. And I can look at him and I can say: Well, he dont *look* like my brother. But there he is. Maybe I better look again.

WHITE. And that's what you did.

BLACK. Well, you was kindly hard to ignore. I got to say that your approach was pretty direct.

WHITE. I didnt approach you. I didnt even see you.

BLACK. Mm hm.

WHITE. I should go. I'm beginning to get on your nerves.

BLACK. No you aint. Dont pay no attention to me. You seem like a sweet man, Professor. I reckon what I dont understand is how come you to get yourself in such a fix.

WHITE. Yeah.

BLACK. Are you okay? Did you sleep last night?

WHITE. No.

BLACK. When did you decide that today was the day? Was they somethin special about it?

WHITE. No. Well. Today is my birthday. But I certainly dont regard that as special.

BLACK. Well happy birthday, Professor.

WHITE. Thank you.

BLACK. So you seen your birthday was comin up and that seemed like the right day.

WHITE. Who knows? Maybe birthdays are dangerous. Like Christmas. Ornaments hanging from the trees, wreaths from the doors, and bodies from the steampipes all over America.

BLACK. Mm. Dont say much for Christmas, does it?

WHITE. Christmas is not what it used to be.

BLACK. I believe that to be a true statement. I surely do.

WHITE. I've got to go. *(He gets up and takes his jacket off the back of the chair and lifts it over his shoulders and then puts his arms in the sleeves rather than putting his arms in first one at a time.)*

BLACK. You always put your coat on like that?

WHITE. What's wrong with the way I put my coat on?

BLACK. I didnt say they was nothin wrong with it. I just wondered if that was your regular method.

WHITE. I dont have a regular method. I just put it on.

BLACK. Mm hm.

WHITE. Its what, effeminate?

BLACK. Mm.

WHITE. What?

BLACK. Nothin. I'm just settin here studyin the ways of professors.

WHITE. Yeah. Well, I've got to go. *(The black gets up.)*

BLACK. Well. Let me get my coat.

WHITE. Your coat?

BLACK. Yeah.

WHITE. Where are you going?

BLACK. Goin with you.

WHITE. What do you mean? Going with me where?

BLACK. Goin with you wherever you goin.

WHITE. No you're not.

BLACK. Yeah I am.

WHITE. I'm going home.

BLACK. All right.

WHITE. All right? You're not going home with me.

BLACK. Sure I am. Let me get my coat.

WHITE. You cant go home with me.

BLACK. Why not?

WHITE. You cant.

BLACK. What. You can go home with me but I cant go home with you?

WHITE. No. I mean no, that's not it. I just need to go home.

BLACK. You live in a apartment?

WHITE. Yes.

BLACK. What. They dont let black folks in there?

WHITE. No. I mean of course they do. Look. No more jokes. I've got to go. I'm very tired.

BLACK. Well I just hope we dont run into no hassle about you gettin me in there.

WHITE. You're serious.

BLACK. Oh I think you know I'm serious.

WHITE. You cant be serious.

BLACK. I'm as serious as a heart attack.

WHITE. Why are you doing this?

BLACK. Me? I aint got no choice in the matter.

WHITE. Of course you have a choice.

BLACK. No I aint.

WHITE. Who appointed you my guardian angel?

BLACK. Let me get my coat.

WHITE. Answer the question.

BLACK. You *know* who appointed me. I didnt ask for you to leap into my arms down in the subway this mornin.

WHITE. I didnt leap into your arms.

BLACK. You didnt?

WHITE. No. I didnt.

BLACK. Well how did you get there then? *(The professor stands with his head lowered. He looks at the chair and then turns and goes and sits down in it.)* What. Now we aint goin?

WHITE. Do you really think that Jesus is in this room?

BLACK. No. I dont *think* he's in this room.

WHITE. You dont?

BLACK. I know he's in this room. *(The professor folds his hands at the table and lowers his head. The black pulls out the other chair and sits again.)* It's the way you put it, Professor. Be like me askin you do you *think* you got your coat on. You see what I'm sayin?

WHITE. It's not the same thing. It's a matter of agreement. If you and I say that I have my coat on and Cecil says that I'm naked and I have green skin and a tail then we might want to think about where we should put Cecil so that he wont hurt himself.

BLACK. Who's Cecil?

WHITE. He's not anybody. He's just a hypothetical ... There's not any Cecil. He's just a person I made up to illustrate a point.

BLACK. Made up.

WHITE. Yes.

BLACK. Mm.

WHITE. We're not going to get into this again are we? It's not the same thing. The fact that I made Cecil up.

BLACK. But you did make him up.

WHITE. Yes.

BLACK. And his view of things dont count.

WHITE. No. That's why I made him up. I could have changed it around. I could have made you the one that didnt think I was wearing a coat.

BLACK. And was green and all that shit you said.

WHITE. Yes.

BLACK. But you didnt.

8

WHITE. No.

BLACK. You loaded it off on Cecil.

WHITE. Yes.

BLACK. But Cecil cant defend hisself cause the fact that he aint in agreement with everbody else makes his word no good. I mean aside from the fact that you made him up and he's green and everthing.

WHITE. He's not the one who's green. I am. Where is this going?

BLACK. I'm just tryin to find out about Cecil.

WHITE. I dont think so. Can you see Jesus?

BLACK. No. I cant see him.

WHITE. But you talk to him.

BLACK. I dont miss a day.

WHITE. And he talks to you.

BLACK. He has talked to me. Yes.

WHITE. Do you hear him? Like out loud?

BLACK. Not out loud. I dont hear a voice. I dont hear my own, for that matter. But I have heard him.

WHITE. Well why couldnt Jesus just be in your head?

BLACK. He is in my head.

WHITE. Well I dont understand what it is that you're trying to tell me.

BLACK. I know you dont, honey. Look. The first thing you got to understand is that I aint got a original thought in my head. If it aint got the lingerin scent of divinity to it then I aint interested.

WHITE. The lingering scent of divinity.

BLACK. Yeah. You like that?

WHITE. It's not bad.

BLACK. I heard it on the radio. Black preacher. But the point is I done tried it the other way. And I dont mean chippied, neither. Runnin blindfold through the woods with the bit tween your teeth. Oh man. Didnt I try it though. If you can find a soul that give it a better shot than me I'd like to meet him. I surely would. And what do you reckon it got me?

WHITE. I dont know. What did it get you?

BLACK. Death in life. That's what it got me.

WHITE. Death in life.

BLACK. Yeah. Walkin around death. Too dead to even know enough to lay down.

WHITE. I see.

BLACK. I dont think so. But let me ask you this question.

WHITE. All right.

BLACK. Have you ever read this book?

WHITE. I've read parts of it. I've read in it.

BLACK. Have you ever read it?

WHITE. I read the *Book of Job*.

BLACK. Have. You. Ever. Read. It.

WHITE. No.

BLACK. But you is read a lot of books.

WHITE. Yes.

BLACK. How many would you say you read?

WHITE. I've no idea.

BLACK. Ball park.

WHITE. I dont know. Two a week maybe. A hundred a year. For close to forty years. *(The black takes up his pencil and licks it and falls to squinting at his pad, adding numbers laboriously, his tongue in the corner of his mouth, one hand on his head.)* Forty times a hundred is four thousand.

BLACK. *(Almost laughing.)* I'm just messin with you, Professor. Give me a number. Any number you like. And I'll give you forty times it back.

WHITE. Twenty-six.

BLACK. A thousand and forty.

WHITE. A hundred and eighteen.

BLACK. Four thousand seven hundred and twenty.

WHITE. Four thousand seven hundred and twenty.

BLACK. Yeah.

WHITE. The answer is the question.

BLACK. Say what?

WHITE. That's your new number.

BLACK. Four thousand seven hundred and twenty?

WHITE. Yes.

BLACK. That's a big number, Professor.

WHITE. Yes it is.

BLACK. Do you know the answer?

WHITE. No. I dont.

BLACK. It's a hundred and eighty-eight thousand and eight hundred. *(They sit.)*

WHITE. Let me have that. *(The black slides the pad and pencil across the table. The professor does the figures and looks at them and looks at the black. He slides the pencil and paper back across the table and sits back.)* How do you do that?

BLACK. Numbers is the black man's friend. Butter and eggs.

10

Crap table. You quick with numbers you can put the mojo on you brother. Confiscate the contents of his pocketbook. You get a lot of time to practice that shit in the jailhouse.

WHITE. I see.

BLACK. But let's get back to all them books you done read. You think maybe you read four thousand books.

WHITE. Probably. Maybe more than that.

BLACK. But you aint read this one.

WHITE. No. Not the whole book. No.

BLACK. Why is that?

WHITE. I dont know.

BLACK. What would you say is the best book that ever was wrote?

WHITE. I have no idea.

BLACK. Take a shot.

WHITE. There are a lot of good books.

BLACK. Well pick one.

WHITE. Maybe *War and Peace*.

BLACK. All right. You think that's a better book than this one?

WHITE. I dont know. They're different kinds of books.

BLACK. This *War and Peace* book. That's a book that somebody made up, right?

WHITE. Well, yes.

BLACK. So is that how it's different from this book?

WHITE. Not really. In my view they're both made up.

BLACK. Mm. Aint neither one of em true.

WHITE. Not in the historical sense. No.

BLACK. So what would be a true book?

WHITE. I suppose maybe a history book. Gibbon's *Decline and Fall of the Roman Empire* might be one. At least the events would be actual events. They would be things that had happened.

BLACK. Mm hm. You think that book is as good a book as this book here?

WHITE. The *Bible*.

BLACK. The *Bible*.

WHITE. I dont know. Gibbon is a cornerstone. It's a major book.

BLACK. And a true book. Dont forget that.

WHITE. And a true book. Yes.

BLACK. But is it as good a book.

WHITE. I dont know. I dont know as you can make a comparison. You're talking about apples and pears.

BLACK. No we aint talkin bout no apples and pears, Professor.

11

We talkin bout books. Is that *Decline and Fall* book as good a book as this book here. Answer the question.

WHITE. I might have to say no.

BLACK. It's more true but it aint as good.

WHITE. If you like.

BLACK. It aint what I like. It's what you said.

WHITE. All right. *(The black lays the Bible back down on the table.)*

BLACK. It used to say here on the cover fore it got wore off: The greatest book ever written. You think that might be true?

WHITE. It might.

BLACK. You read good books.

WHITE. I try to. Yes.

BLACK. But not the best book. Why is that?

WHITE. I need to go.

BLACK. You dont need to go, Professor. Stay here and visit with me.

WHITE. You're afraid I'll go back to the train station.

BLACK. You might. Just stay with me.

WHITE. What if I promised I wouldnt?

BLACK. You might anyways.

WHITE. Dont you have to go to work?

BLACK. I was on my way to work.

WHITE. A funny thing happened to you on your way to work.

BLACK. Yes it did.

WHITE. Will they fire you?

BLACK. Naw. They aint goin fire me.

WHITE. You could call in.

BLACK. Aint got a phone. Anyways, they know if I aint there I aint comin. I aint a late sort of person.

WHITE. Why dont you have a phone?

BLACK. I dont need one. The junkies'd steal it anyways.

WHITE. You could get a cheap one.

BLACK. You cant get too cheap for a junky. But let's get back to you.

WHITE. Let's stick with you for a minute.

BLACK. All right.

WHITE. Can I ask you something?

BLACK. Sure you can.

WHITE. Where were you standing? I never saw you.

BLACK. You mean when you took your amazin leap?

WHITE. Yes.

BLACK. I was on the platform.

WHITE. On the platform.

BLACK. Yeah.

WHITE. Well I didnt see you.

BLACK. I was just standin there on the platform. Mindin my own business. And here you come. Haulin ass.

WHITE. I'd looked all around to make sure there was no one there. Particularly no children. There was nobody around.

BLACK. Nope. Just me.

WHITE. Well I dont know where you could have been.

BLACK. Mm. Professor you fixin to get spooky on me now. Maybe I was behind a post or somethin.

WHITE. There wasnt any post.

BLACK. So what are we sayin here? You lookin at some big black angel got sent down here to grab your honky ass out of the air at the last possible minute and save you from destruction?

WHITE. No. I dont think that.

BLACK. Such a thing aint possible.

WHITE. No. It isnt.

BLACK. Well you the one suggested it.

WHITE. I didnt suggest any such thing. You're the one put in the stuff about angels. I never said anything about angels. I dont believe in angels.

BLACK. What is it you believe in?

WHITE. A lot of things.

BLACK. All right.

WHITE. All right what?

BLACK. All right what things.

WHITE. I believe in things.

BLACK. You said that.

WHITE. Probably I dont believe in a lot of things that I used to believe in but that doesnt mean I dont believe in anything.

BLACK. Well give me a for instance.

WHITE. Mostly the value of things.

BLACK. Value of things.

WHITE. Yes.

BLACK. Okay. What things.

WHITE. Lots of things. Cultural things, for instance. Books and music and art. Things like that.

BLACK. All right.

WHITE. Those are the kinds of things that have value to me. They're the foundations of civilization. Or they used to have value. I suppose they dont have so much any more.

BLACK. What happened to em?

WHITE. People stopped valuing them. I stopped valuing them. To a certain extent. I'm not sure I could tell you why. That world is largely gone. Soon it will be wholly gone.

BLACK. I aint sure I'm followin you, Professor.

WHITE. There's nothing to follow. It's all right. The things that I loved were very frail. Very fragile. I didnt know that. I thought they were indestructible. They werent.

BLACK. And that's what sent you off the edge of the platform. It wasnt nothin personal.

WHITE. It is personal. That's what an education does. It makes the world personal.

BLACK. Hm.

WHITE. Hm what.

BLACK. Well. I was just thinkin that them is some pretty powerful words. I dont know that I got a answer about any of that and it might be that they aint no answer. But still I got to ask what is the use of notions such as them if it wont keep you glued down to the platform when the Sunset Limited comes through at eighty mile a hour.

WHITE. Good question.

BLACK. I thought so.

WHITE. I dont have an answer to any of that either. Maybe it's not logical. I dont know. I dont care. I've been asked didnt I think it odd that I should be present to witness the death of everything and I do think it's odd but that doesnt mean it's not so. Someone has to be here.

BLACK. But you dont intend to stick around for it.

WHITE. No. I dont.

BLACK. So let me see if I got this straight. You sayin that all this culture stuff is all they ever was tween you and the Sunset Limited.

WHITE. It's a lot.

BLACK. But it busted out on you.

WHITE. Yes.

BLACK. You a culture junky.

WHITE. If you like. Or I was. Maybe you're right. Maybe I have no beliefs. I believe in the Sunset Limited.

BLACK. Damn, Professor.

WHITE. Damn indeed.

BLACK. No beliefs.

WHITE. The things I believed in dont exist any more. It's foolish to pretend that they do. Western Civilization finally went up in smoke in the chimneys at Dachau but I was too infatuated to see it. I see it now.

BLACK. You a challenge, Professor. Did you know that?

WHITE. Well, there's no reason for you to become involved in my problems. I should go.

BLACK. You got any friends?

WHITE. No.

BLACK. You aint got even one friend?

WHITE. No.

BLACK. You got to be kiddin me, Professor. Not one?

WHITE. Not really. No.

BLACK. Well tell me about that one.

WHITE. What one?

BLACK. The not really one.

WHITE. I have a friend at the university. Not a close friend. We have lunch from time to time.

BLACK. But that's about as good as it gets.

WHITE. What do you mean?

BLACK. That's about all you got in the way of friends.

WHITE. Yes.

BLACK. Mm. Well. If that's the best friend you got then I reckon that's your best friend. Aint it?

WHITE. I dont know.

BLACK. What did you do to him.

WHITE. What did I do to him?

BLACK. Yeah.

WHITE. I didnt do anything to him.

BLACK. Mm hm.

WHITE. I didnt do anything to him. What makes you think I did something to him?

BLACK. I dont know. Did you?

WHITE. No. What is it you think I did to him?

BLACK. I dont know. I'm waitin on you to tell me.

WHITE. Well there's nothing to tell.

BLACK. But you didnt leave him no note or nothin. When you decided to take the train.

WHITE. No.

BLACK. Your best friend?

WHITE. He's not my best friend.

BLACK. I thought we just got done decidin that he was.

WHITE. *You* just got done deciding.

BLACK. You ever tell him you was thinkin about this?

WHITE. No.

BLACK. Damn, Professor.

WHITE. Why should I?

BLACK. I dont know. Maybe cause he's your best friend?

WHITE. I told you. We're not all that close.

BLACK. Not all that close.

WHITE. No.

BLACK. He's your best friend only you aint all that close.

WHITE. If you like.

BLACK. Not to where you'd want to bother him about a little thing like dyin.

WHITE. *(Looking around the room.)* Look. Suppose I were to give you my word that I would just go home and that I wouldnt try to kill myself en route.

BLACK. Suppose I was to give you my word that I wouldnt listen to none of your bullshit.

WHITE. So what am I, a prisoner here?

BLACK. You know better n that. Anyway, you was a prisoner fore you got here. Death Row prisoner. What did your daddy do?

WHITE. What?

BLACK. I said what did your daddy do. What kind of work.

WHITE. He was a lawyer.

BLACK. Lawyer.

WHITE. Yes.

BLACK. What kind of law did he do?

WHITE. He was a government lawyer. He didnt do criminal law or things like that.

BLACK. Mmhm. What would be a thing *like* criminal law?

WHITE. I dont know. Divorce law, maybe.

BLACK. Yeah. Maybe you got a point. What did he die of?

WHITE. Who said he was dead?

BLACK. Is he dead?

WHITE. Yes.

BLACK. What did he die of?

WHITE. Cancer.

BLACK. Cancer. So he was sick for a while.

WHITE. Yes. He was.

BLACK. Did you go see him?

WHITE. No.

BLACK. How come?

WHITE. I didnt want to.

BLACK. Well how come you didnt want to?

WHITE. I dont know. I just didnt. Maybe I didnt want to remember him that way.

BLACK. Bullshit. Did he ask you to come?

WHITE. No.

BLACK. But your mama did.

WHITE. She may have. I dont remember.

BLACK. Come on, Professor. She asked you to come.

WHITE. Okay. Yes.

BLACK. And what did you tell her?

WHITE. I told her I would.

BLACK. But you didnt.

WHITE. No.

BLACK. How come?

WHITE. He died.

BLACK. Yeah; but that aint it. You had time to go see him and you didnt do it.

WHITE. I suppose.

BLACK. You waited till he was dead.

WHITE. Okay. So I didnt go and see my father.

BLACK. Your daddy is layin on his deathbed dyin of cancer. Your mama settin there with him. Holdin his hand. He in all kinds of pain. And they ask you to come see him one last time fore he dies and you tell em no. You aint comin. Please tell me I got some part of this wrong.

WHITE. If that's the way you want to put it.

BLACK. Well how would you put it?

WHITE. I dont know.

BLACK. That's the way it is. Aint it?

WHITE. I suppose.

BLACK. No you dont suppose. Is it or aint it?

WHITE. Yes.

BLACK. Well. Let me see if I can find my train schedule. *(He opens the table drawer and rummages through it.)* See when that next uptown express is due.

WHITE. I'm not sure I see the humor.

BLACK. I'm glad to hear you say that, Professor. Cause I aint sure either. I just get more amazed by the minute, that's all. How come you cant *see* yourself, honey? You plain as glass. I can see the wheels turnin in there. The gears. And I can see the light too. Good light.

True light. Cant you see it?

WHITE. No. I cant.

BLACK. Well bless you, brother. Bless you and keep you. Cause it's there. *(They sit.)*

WHITE. When were you in the penitentiary?

BLACK. Long time ago.

WHITE. What were you in for?

BLACK. Murder.

WHITE. Really?

BLACK. Now who would claim to be a murderer that wasnt one?

WHITE. You called it the jailhouse.

BLACK. Yeah?

WHITE. Do most blacks call the penitentiary the jailhouse?

BLACK. Naw. Just us old country niggers. We kind of make it a point to call things for what they is. I'd hate to guess how many names they is for the jailhouse. I'd hate to have to count em.

WHITE. Do you have a lot of jailhouse stories?

BLACK. Jailhouse stories.

WHITE. Yes.

BLACK. I dont know. I used to tell jailhouse stories some but they kindly lost their charm. Maybe we ought to talk about somethin more cheerful.

WHITE. Have you ever been married?

BLACK. Married.

WHITE. Yes.

BLACK. *(Softly.)* Oh man.

WHITE. What.

BLACK. Maybe we ought to take another look at them jailhouse stories. *(He shakes his head, laughing soundlessly. He pinches the bridge of his nose, his eyes shut.)* Oh my.

WHITE. Do you have any children?

BLACK. Naw, Professor, I aint got nobody. Everbody in my family is dead. I had two boys. They been dead for years. Just about everbody I ever knowed is dead, far as that goes. You might want to think about that. I might be a hazard to your health.

WHITE. You were always in a lot of trouble?

BLACK. Yeah. I was. I liked it. Maybe I still do. I done seven years hard time and I was lucky not to of done a lot more. I hurt a lot of people. I'd smack em around a little and then they wouldnt get up again.

WHITE. But you dont get in trouble now.

18

BLACK. No.

WHITE. But you still like it?

BLACK. Well, maybe I'm just condemned to it. Bit in the ass by my own karma. But I'm on the other side now. You want to help people that's in trouble you pretty much got to go where the trouble is at. You aint got a lot of choice.

WHITE. And you want to help people in trouble.

BLACK. Yeah.

WHITE. Why is that? *(The black tilts his head and studies him.)*

BLACK. You aint ready for that.

WHITE. How about just the short answer.

BLACK. That is the short answer.

WHITE. How long have you been here?

BLACK. You mean in this buildin?

WHITE. Yes.

BLACK. Six years. Seven, almost.

WHITE. I dont understand why you live here.

BLACK. As compared to where?

WHITE. Anywhere.

BLACK. Well I'd say this pretty much is anywhere. I could live in another buildin I reckon. This is all right. I got a bedroom where I can get away. Got a sofa yonder where people can crash. Junkies and crackheads, mostly. Of course they goin to carry off your portables so I dont own nothin. And that's good. You hang out with the right crowd and you'll finally get cured of just about ever cravin. They took the refrigerator one time but somebody caught em on the stairs with it and made em bring it back up. Now I got that big sucker yonder. Traded up. Only thing I miss is the music. I aim to get me a steel door for the bedroom. Then I can have me some music again. You got to get the door and the frame together. I'm workin on that. I dont care nothin about television but I miss that music.

WHITE. You dont think this is a terrible place?

BLACK. Terrible?

WHITE. Yes.

BLACK. What's terrible about it?

WHITE. It's horrible. It's a horrible life.

BLACK. Horrible life?

WHITE. Yes.

BLACK. Damn, Professor. This aint a horrible life. What you talkin bout?

WHITE. This place. It's a horrible place. Full of horrible people.

BLACK. Oh my.

WHITE. You must know these people are not worth saving. Even if they could be saved. Which they cant. You must know that.

BLACK. Well, I always liked a challenge. I started a ministry in prison fore I got out. Now that was a challenge. Lot of the brothers'd show up that they didnt really care nothin bout it. They couldnt of cared less bout the word of God. They just wanted it on their resumé.

WHITE. Resumé?

BLACK. Resumé. You had brothers in there that had done some real bad shit and they wasnt sorry about a damn thing cept gettin caught. Of course the funny thing was a lot of em did believe in God. Maybe even more than these folks here on the outside. I know I did. You might want to think about that, Professor.

WHITE. I think I'd better go.

BLACK. You dont need to go, Professor. What am I goin to do, you leave me settin here by myself?

WHITE. You dont need me. You just dont want to feel responsible if anything happens to me.

BLACK. What's the difference?

WHITE. I dont know. I just need to go.

BLACK. Just stay a while. This place is got to be more cheerful than you own.

WHITE. I dont think you have any idea how strange it is for me to be here.

BLACK. I think I got some idea.

WHITE. I have to go.

BLACK. Let me ask you somethin.

WHITE. All right.

BLACK. You ever had one of them days when things was just sort of weird all the way around? When things just kindly fell into place?

WHITE. I'm not sure what you mean.

BLACK. Just one of them days. Just kind of magic. One of them days when everthing turns out right.

WHITE. I dont know. Maybe. Why?

BLACK. I just wondered if maybe it aint been kindly a long dry spell for you. Until you finally took up with the notion that that's the way the world is.

WHITE. The way the world is.

BLACK. Yeah.

WHITE. And how is that?

BLACK. I dont know. Long and dry. The point is that even if it might seem that way to you you still got to understand that the sun dont shine up the same dog's ass ever day. You understand what I'm sayin?

WHITE. If what you're saying is that I'm simply having a bad day that's ridiculous.

BLACK. I dont think you havin a bad day, Professor. I think you havin a bad life.

WHITE. You think I should change my life.

BLACK. What, are you shittin me?

WHITE. I have to go.

BLACK. You could hang with me here a little while longer.

WHITE. What about my jailhouse story?

BLACK. You dont need to hear no jailhouse story.

WHITE. Why not?

BLACK. Well, you kind of suspicious bout everthing. You think I'm fixin to put you in the trick bag.

WHITE. And you're not.

BLACK. Oh no. I am. I just dont want you to know about it.

WHITE. Well, in any case I need to go.

BLACK. You know you aint ready to hit the street.

WHITE. I have to.

BLACK. I know you aint got nothin you got to do.

WHITE. And how do you know that?

BLACK. Cause you aint even supposed to be here.

WHITE. I see your point.

BLACK. What if I was to tell you a jailhouse story? You stay then?

WHITE. All right. I'll stay for a while.

BLACK. My man. All right. Here's my jailhouse story.

WHITE. Is it a true story?

BLACK. Oh yeah. It's a true story. I dont know no other kind.

WHITE. All right.

BLACK. All right. I'm in the chowline and I'm gettin my chow and this nigger in the line behind me gets into it with the server. Says the beans is cold and he throws the ladle down in the beans. And when he done that they was beans splashed on me. Well, I wasnt goin to get into it over some beans but it did piss me off some. I'd just put on a clean suit — you know, khakis, shirt and trousers — and you only got two a week. And I did say somethin to him like Hey man, watch it, or somethin like that. But I went on, and I'm thinkin, just let it go. Let it go. And then this dude says somethin to me and I turned and looked back at him and when I done that he stuck a knife in me. I never even seen it. And the blood is just flyin. And this aint no jailhouse shiv neither. It's one of them Italian switchblades. One of them black and silver jobs. And I didnt do a thing in the world but duck and step under the rail and I reached and got hold of the leg of this table and it come off in my hand just as easy. And it's got this big long screw stickin out of the end of it and I went to wailin on this nigger's head and I didnt quit. I beat on it till you couldnt hardly tell it was a head. And that screw'd stick in his head and I'd have to stand on him to pull it out again.

WHITE. What did he say?

BLACK. What did he say?

WHITE. I mean in the line. What did he say.

BLACK. I aint goin to repeat it.

WHITE. That doesnt seem fair.

BLACK. Dont seem fair.

WHITE. No.

BLACK. Hm. Well, here I'm tellin you a bonafide blood and guts tale from the Big House. The genuine article. And I cant get you to fill in the blanks about what this nigger said?

WHITE. Do you have to use that word?

BLACK. Use that word.

WHITE. Yes.

BLACK. We aint makin much progress here, is we?

WHITE. It just seems unnecessary.

BLACK. You dont want to hear nigger but you about to bail out on me on account of I wont tell you some terrible shit the nigger said. You sure about this?

WHITE. I just dont see why you have to say that word.

BLACK. Well it's my story aint it? Anyway I dont remember there bein no Afro-Americans or persons of color there. To the best of my recollection it was just a bunch of niggers.

WHITE. Go ahead.

BLACK. Well at some point I had pulled the knife out and I reckon I'd done dropped it in the floor. I'm wailin on this nigger's head and all the time I'm doin that his buddy has got hold of me from behind. But I'm holdin on to the rail with one hand and I aint goin nowhere. Course what I dont know is that this other dude has picked up the knife and he's tryin to gut me with it. I finally felt the blood and I turned around and busted him in the head and he went skitterin off across the floor, and by now they done pushed the button and the alarm is goin and everbody's down on the floor and we're in lockdown and the guard up on the tier is got a shotgun pointed at me and he hollers at me to put down my weapon and get on the floor. And he's about to shoot me when the lieutenant comes in and hollers at him to hold his fire and he tells me to throw that club down and I looked around and I'm the only one standin. I seen the nigger's feet stickin out from under the servin counter where he'd crawled so I throwed the thing down and I dont remember much after that. They told me I'd lost about half my blood. I remember slippin around in it but I thought it was this other dude's.

WHITE. *(Dryly.)* That's quite a story.

BLACK. Yeah. That's really just the introduction to the actual story.

WHITE. Did the man die?

BLACK. No he didnt. Everybody lived. They thought he was dead but he wasnt. He never was right after that so I never had no more trouble out of him. He was missin a eye and he walked around with his head sort of sideways and one arm hangin down. Couldnt talk right. They finally shipped him off to another facility.

WHITE. But that's not the whole story.

BLACK. No. It aint.

WHITE. So what happened.

BLACK. I woke up in the infirmary. They had done operated on me. My spleen was cut open. Liver. I dont know what all. I come pretty close to dyin. And I had two hundred and eighty stitches holdin me together and I was hurtin. I didnt know you could hurt that bad. And still they got me in leg irons and got me handcuffed to the bed. If you can believe that. And I'm layin there and I hear this voice. Just as clear. Couldnt of been no clearer. And this voice says: If it was not for the grace of God you would not be here. Man. I tried to raise up and look around but of course I couldnt move. Wasnt no need to anyways. They wasnt nobody there. I mean, they was somebody there all right but they wasnt no use in me lookin around to see if I could see him.

WHITE. You dont think this is a strange kind of story?

BLACK. I do think it's a strange kind of story.

WHITE. What I mean is that you didnt feel sorry for this man?

BLACK. You gettin ahead of the story.

WHITE. The story of how a fellow prisoner became a crippled one-eyed halfwit so that you could find God.

BLACK. Whoa.

WHITE. Well isnt it?

BLACK. I dont know.

WHITE. You hadnt thought of it that way.

BLACK. Oh I'd thought of it that way.

WHITE. And?

BLACK. And what?

WHITE. Isnt that the real story?

BLACK. Well. I dont want to get on the wrong side of you. You seem to have a powerful wish for that to be the real story. So I will say that that is certainly one way to look at it. I got to concede that. I got to keep you interested.

WHITE. String me along.

BLACK. That okay with you?

WHITE. And then put me in the what was it? The trick bag?

BLACK. Yeah.

WHITE. Right.

BLACK. You got to remember this is a jailhouse story.

WHITE. All right.

BLACK. Which you specifically asked for.

WHITE. All right.

BLACK. The point is, Professor, that I aint got the first notion in the world about what makes God tick. I dont know why he spoke to me. I wouldnt of.

WHITE. But you listened.

BLACK. Well what choice would you have?

WHITE. I dont know Not listen?

BLACK. How you goin to do that?

WHITE. Just dont listen.

BLACK. Do you think he goes around talkin to people that he knows aint goin to listen in the first place? You think he's got that kind of free time?

WHITE. I see your point.

BLACK. If he didnt know I was ready to listen he wouldnt of said a word.

WHITE. He's an opportunist.

BLACK. Meanin I guess that he seen somebody in a place low enough to where he ought to be ready to take a pretty big step.

WHITE. Something like that.

BLACK. And you think that maybe I think that you might be in somethin like that kind of a place you own self.

WHITE. Could be.

BLACK. Well I can dig that. I can dig it. Of course they is one small problem.

WHITE. And that is.

BLACK. I aint God.

WHITE. I'm glad to hear you say that.

BLACK. It come as a relief to me too.

WHITE. Did you used to think you were God?

BLACK. No. I didnt. I didnt know what I was. But I thought I was in charge. I never knowed what that burden weighed till I put it down. That might of been the sweetest thing of all. To just hand over the keys.

WHITE. Let me ask you something.

BLACK. Ask it.

WHITE. Why cant you people just accept it that some people dont even *want* to believe in God.

BLACK. I accept that.

WHITE. You do?

BLACK. Sure I do. Meanin that I believe it to be a fact. I'm lookin at it ever day. I better accept it.

WHITE. Then why cant you leave us alone?

BLACK. To do your own thing.

WHITE. Yes.

BLACK. Hangin from them steampipes and all.

WHITE. If that's what we want to do, yes.

BLACK. Cause he said not to. It's in here. *(Holding up the book. The professor shakes his head.)* I guess you dont want to be happy.

WHITE. Happy?

BLACK. Yeah. What's wrong with happy?

WHITE. God help us.

BLACK. What. We done opened a can of worms here? What you got against bein happy?

WHITE. It's contrary to the human condition.

BLACK. Well. It's contrary to your condition. I got to agree with that.

WHITE. Happy. This is ridiculous.

BLACK. Like they aint no such a thing.

WHITE. No.

BLACK. Not for nobody.

WHITE. No.

BLACK. Mm. How'd we get in such a fix as this?

WHITE. We were born in such a fix as this. Suffering and human destiny are the same thing. Each is a description of the other.

BLACK. We aint talkin about sufferin. We talkin about bein happy.

WHITE. Well you cant be happy if you're in pain.

BLACK. Why not?

WHITE. You're not making any sense. *(The black falls back clutching his chest.)*

BLACK. Oh them is some hard words from the professor. The preacher has fell back. He's clutchin his heart. Eyes is rolled back in his head. Wait a minute. Wait a minute folks. His eyes is blinkin. I think he's comin back. I think he's comin back. *(The black sits up and leans forward.)* The point, Professor, is that if you didnt have no pain in your life then how would you even know you *was* happy? As compared to what?

WHITE. You dont have anything to drink around here do you?

BLACK. No, Professor, I aint. You a drinkin man?

WHITE. Are we about to get a temperance lecture?

BLACK. Not from me.

WHITE. It's been a difficult day. I take it you dont drink.

BLACK. I dont. I have done my share of it in my time.

WHITE. Are you in AA?

BLACK. No. No AA. I just quit. I've had a lots of friends was drinkers. Most of em, for that matter. Most of em dead, too.

WHITE. From drinking.

BLACK. Well. From drinkin or from reasons that dont get too far from drinkin. Not too long ago I had a friend to get run down by a taxicab. Now where do you reckon he was goin? Drunk.

WHITE. I dont know. Where was he going?

BLACK. Goin after more whiskey. Had plenty at the house. But a drunk is always afraid of runnin out.

WHITE. Was he killed?

BLACK. I hope so. We buried him.

WHITE. I suppose there's a moral to this story.

BLACK. Well, it's just a story about what you want and what you get. Pain and happiness. I'll tell you another one.

WHITE. All right.

BLACK. One Sunday they's a bunch of us settin around at my house drinkin. Sunday mornin. Favorite time for drunks to get together and drink and I'll let you think about why that might be so. Well here come one of my buddies with this girl. Evelyn. And Evelyn was drunk when she got there but we fixed her a drink and directly Redge — my buddy — he goes back in the kitchen to get him a drink only now the bottle's gone. Well, Redge has been around a few drinkin people in his time so he commences to hunt for the bottle. Looks in all the cabinets and behind everthing. He cant find it but of course he knows what's happened to it so he comes back in and he sets down and he looks at Miss Evelyn settin there on the sofa. Drunk as a goat. And he says: Evelyn, where's the whiskey? And Evelyn, she goes: Ah ghaga baba lala ghaga. And he says: Evelyn, where did you put the whiskey? Ah lala bloggleblabla. And Redge is settin there and this is beginnin' to piss him off just a little and he gets in her face and he goes: Ah loddle loddle blabble ghaga blabla and she says I hid it in the toilet.

WHITE. That's pretty funny.

BLACK. I thought you might like that.

WHITE. And is that where the whiskey was?

BLACK. Oh yeah. That's a favorite place for drunks to hide a bottle. But the point of course is that the drunk's concern aint that he's goin to die from drinkin — which he is. It's that he's goin to run out of whiskey fore he gets a chance to do it. Are you hungry? I can come back to this. I aint goin to lose my place.

WHITE. I'm all right. Go ahead.

BLACK. If you was to hand a drunk a drink and tell him he really dont want it what do you reckon he'd say?

WHITE. I think I know what he'd say.

BLACK. Sure you do. But you'd still be right.

WHITE. About him not really wanting it.

BLACK. Yes. Because what he really wants he cant get. Or he thinks he cant get it. So what he really dont want he cant get enough of.

WHITE. So what is it that he really wants.

BLACK. You know what he really wants.

WHITE. No I dont.

BLACK. Yeah you do.

WHITE. No I dont.

BLACK. Hm.

WHITE. Hm what.

BLACK. You a hard case, Professor.

WHITE. You're not exactly a day at the beach yourself.

BLACK. You dont know what he wants.

WHITE. No. I do not.

BLACK. He wants what everbody wants.

WHITE. And that is?

BLACK. He wants to be loved by God.

WHITE. I dont want to be loved by God.

BLACK. I love that. See how you cut right to it? He dont either. Accordin to him. He just wants a drink of whiskey. You a smart man, Professor. You tell me which one makes sense and which one dont.

WHITE. I dont want a drink of whiskey, either.

BLACK. I thought you just got done askin for one?

WHITE. I mean as a general proposition.

BLACK. We aint talkin' about no general propositions. We talkin' about a drink.

WHITE. I dont have a drinking problem.

BLACK. Well you got some kind of a problem.

WHITE. Well whatever kind of a problem I have it's not something that I imagine can be addressed with a drink of liquor.

BLACK. Mm. I love the way you put that. So what can it be addressed with?

WHITE. I think you know what it can be addressed with.

BLACK. The Sunset Limited.

WHITE. Yes.

BLACK. And that's what you want.

WHITE. That's what I want. Yes.

BLACK. That's a mighty big drink of whiskey, Professor.

WHITE. That I dont really want.

BLACK. That you dont really want. Yes.

WHITE. Well. I think I do want it.

BLACK. Of course you do, honey. If you didnt we wouldnt be settin here.

WHITE. Well. I disagree with you.

BLACK. That's all right. That's the hand I'm playin.

WHITE. I dont think you understand that people such as myself see a yearning for God as something lacking in those people.

BLACK. I do understand that. Couldnt agree more.

WHITE. You agree with that?

BLACK. Sure I do. What's lackin is God.

WHITE. Well, as I say, we'll just have to disagree.

BLACK. You aint closin down the forum for discussion are you?

WHITE. Not at this juncture.

BLACK. Cause I had a little more to say.

WHITE. How did I know that?

BLACK. I did go to one or two AA meetins. Lot of folks didnt like the God part of it all that much but I hadnt set there too long fore I figured out that the God part was really all the part they was. The problem wasnt that they was too much God in AA it was that they wasnt enough. And I got a pretty thick head about some things but I finally figured out that what was true about AA was probably true about a lot of other things too.

WHITE. Well I'm sorry, but to me the whole idea of God is just a load of crap. *(The black puts his hand to his chest and leans back.)*

BLACK. Oh Lord have mercy oh save us Jesus. The professor's done blasphemed all over us. We aint never gone be saved now. *(He closes his eyes and shakes his head, laughing silently.)*

WHITE. You dont find that an evil thing to say.

BLACK. Oh mercy. No, Professor. I dont. But you does.

WHITE. No I dont. It's simply a fact.

BLACK. No it aint no simply a fact. It's the biggest fact about you. It's just about the only fact.

WHITE. But you dont seem to think that it's so bad.

BLACK. Well, I know it to be curable. So it aint *that* bad. If you talkin about what that man up there thinks about it I figure he's probably seen enough of it that it dont bother him as bad as you might think. I mean, what if somebody told you that you didnt exist. And you settin' there listenin' to him say it. That wouldnt really piss you off, would it?

WHITE. No. You'd just feel sorry for them.

BLACK. I think that's right. You might even try to get some help for em. Now in my case he had to holler at me out loud and me layin on a slab in two pieces that they'd sewed back together where some nigger done tried to core me like a apple but still I got to say that if God is God then he can speak to your heart at any time and furthermore I got to say that if he spoke to me — which he did — then he can speak to anybody. *(The black drums his fingers lightly three times on the table and looks at the professor. Silence.)* Well. Wonder what this crazy nigger fixin to do. He liable to put the mojo on me. Be speakin in tongues here directly. I better get my ass out of here. He's liable to try and steal my pocketbook. Need to get my ass down to the train depot fore somethin happen to me. What we goin to do with you, Professor?

WHITE. I need to go.

BLACK. I thought you was goin to stay and visit with me some.

WHITE. Look. I know I owe you a good deal. In the eyes of the world at least. Cant I just give you something and we'll call it square? I could give you some money. Something like that. *(The black studies him. He doesnt answer.)* I could give you a thousand dollars. Well. That's not very much, I guess. I could give you three

29

thousand, say.

BLACK. You dont have no notion the trouble you in, do you?

WHITE. I dont know what you mean.

BLACK. I know you dont.

WHITE. I'd just like to settle this someway.

BLACK. It aint me you got to settle with.

WHITE. Do you really believe I was sent to you by God?

BLACK. Oh it's worse than that.

WHITE. How do you mean?

BLACK. Belief aint like unbelief. If you a believer then you got to come finally to the well of belief itself and then you dont have to look no further. There aint no further. But the unbeliever has got a problem. He has set out to unravel the world, but everthing he can point to that aint true leaves two new things layin there. If God walked the earth when he got done makin it then when you get up in the mornin' you get to put your feet on a real floor and you dont have to worry about where it come from. But if he didnt then you got to come up with a whole other description of what you even mean by real. And you got to judge everthing by that same light. If light it is. Includin yourself. One question fits all. So what do you think, Professor? Is you real?

WHITE. I'm not buying it.

BLACK. That's all right. It's been on the market a long time and it'll be there a while yet.

WHITE. Do you believe everything that's in there? In the Bible?

BLACK. The literal truth?

WHITE. Yes.

BLACK. Probably not. But then you already know I'm a outlaw.

WHITE. What is it you would disagree with?

BLACK. Maybe the notion of original sin. When Eve eat the apple and it turned everbody bad. I dont see people that way. I think for the most part people are good to start with. I think evil is somethin you bring on your own self. Mostly from wantin' what you aint supposed to have. But I aint goin to set here and tell you about me bein a heretic when I'm tryin to get you to quit bein one.

WHITE. Are you a heretic?

BLACK. You tryin to put me in the trick bag, Professor.

WHITE. No I'm not. Are you?

BLACK. No more than what a man should be. Even a man with a powerful belief. I aint a doubter. But I am a questioner.

WHITE. What's the difference?

BLACK. Well, I think the questioner wants the truth. The doubter wants to be told there aint no such thing.

WHITE. *(Pointing at Bible.)* You dont think you have to believe everything in there in order to be saved?

BLACK. No. I dont. I dont think you even have to read it. I aint for sure you even got to know there is such a book. I think whatever truth is wrote in these pages is wrote in the human heart too and it was wrote there a long time ago and will still be wrote there a long time hence. Even if this book is burned ever copy of it. What Jesus said? I dont think he made up a word of it. I think he just told it. This book is a guide for the ignorant and the sick at heart. A whole man wouldnt need it at all. And of course if you read this book you goin to find that they's a lot more talk in here about the wrong way than they is about the right way. Now why is that?

WHITE. I dont know. Why is it?

BLACK. I'd rather hear from you.

WHITE. I'll have to think about it.

BLACK. Okay. *(Silence.)*

WHITE. Okay what?

BLACK. Okay go ahead and think about it.

WHITE. It might take me a little longer than you to think about something.

BLACK. That's all right.

WHITE. That's all right.

BLACK. Yes. I mean they's two ways you can take that remark but I'm goin to take it the good way. It's just my nature. That way I get to live in my world instead of yours.

WHITE. What makes you think mine's so bad?

BLACK. Oh I dont know as it's so bad. I know it's brief.

WHITE. All right. Are you ready?

BLACK. I'm ready.

WHITE. I think the answer to your question is that the dialectic of the homily always presupposes a ground of evil.

BLACK. Man.

WHITE. How's that.

BLACK. That's strong as a mare's breath, Professor. Wouldnt I love to lay some of that shit on the brothers? Whoa. Now. Just the two of us here talkin. In private. What did you just say?

WHITE. Your question. The Bible is full of cautionary tales. All of literature, for that matter. Telling us to be careful. Careful of what? Taking a wrong turn. A wrong path. How many wrong paths are there? Their number is legion. How many right paths? Only one. Hence the imbalance you spoke of.

BLACK. Man. I'll tell you what, Professor. You could go on television. Goodlookin man such as yourself. Did you know that?

WHITE. Stop.

BLACK. I'm serious. I wasnt even all that sure you *was* a professor till you laid that shit on me.

WHITE. I think you're having fun at my expense.

BLACK. Aint done no such a thing, Professor.

WHITE. Well. I think you are.

BLACK. Honey, I swear I aint. I couldnt say a thing like you just got done sayin. I admire that.

WHITE. And why do you keep calling me honey?

BLACK. That's just the old south talkin. They aint nothin wrong with it. I'll try and quit if it bothers you.

WHITE. I'm just not sure what it means.

BLACK. It means you among friends. It means quit worryin bout everthing.

WHITE. That might be easier said than done.

BLACK. Well yes it might. But we just talkin here. Just talkin.

WHITE. What else?

BLACK. What else what?

WHITE. Any other heresies?

BLACK. At this juncture?

WHITE. At this juncture. Yes.

BLACK. Yeah, but I aint tellin you.

WHITE. Why not?

BLACK. Cause I aint. Shouldnt of told you what I did.

WHITE. Why not?

BLACK. You settin here at my table dead to God as the fallen angels and you waitin on me to lay another heresy on you to clutch to your bosom and help shore you up in your infidelity and I aint goin to do it. That's all.

WHITE. Dont then.

BLACK. Dont worry. I aint.

WHITE. I have to go.

BLACK. Ever time the dozens gets a little heavy you got to go.

WHITE. What's the dozens?

BLACK. It aint really even the dozens. It's really just a discussion.

WHITE. What's the dozens.

BLACK. It's when two of the brothers stands around insultin one another and the first one gets pissed off loses.

WHITE. What is the point of it?

BLACK. Winnin and losin is the point of it. Same as the point of everthing else.

WHITE. And you win by making the other guy angry.

BLACK. That's correct.

WHITE. I dont get it.

BLACK. You aint supposed to get it. You white.

WHITE. Then why did you tell me?

BLACK. Cause you asked me.

WHITE. So if I find you a bit irritating and decide to leave then I lose.

BLACK. Well, like I said, this aint even the dozens. We just talkin.

WHITE. But that's what you think.

BLACK. Oh yeah, that's what I think.

WHITE. Well how long do you think I might have to stay before I could leave without losing?

BLACK. That's kindly hard to say. I guess the best way to put it might be that you'd have to stay till you didnt want to leave.

WHITE. Stay until I didnt want to leave.

BLACK. Yeah.

WHITE. And then I could leave.

BLACK. Yeah. (*The professor runs one hand alongside his head and then holds the back of his neck, his head down and his eyes closed. He looks up.*)

WHITE. Why is it called the dozens?

BLACK. Dont know.

WHITE. What sorts of insults?

BLACK. Oh, you might say somethin about the other man's mama. That's a sensitive area, you might say. And he might lose it and come after your ass but when he done that it's like he's sayin that what you just got done tellin about his mama was true. It's like he sayin: You aint supposed to know that about my mama and you damn sure aint supposed to of told it and now I'm fixin to whip your ass. You see what I'm sayin?

WHITE. I suppose.

BLACK. Well, probably not.

WHITE. And is this something you do with your friends?

BLACK. Me? No. I dont play the dozens.

WHITE. Tell me something.

BLACK. Sure.

WHITE. Why are you here? What do you get out of this? You seem like a smart man.

BLACK. Me? I'm just a dumb country nigger from Louisiana. I done told you. I aint never had the first thought in my head. If it aint in here then I dont know it. (*He holds the Bible up off the table and lays it down again.*)

WHITE. Half the time I think you're having fun with me. I dont see how you can live here. I dont see how you can feel safe.

BLACK. Well you got a point, Professor. About bein safe anyways.

WHITE. Have you ever stopped any of these people from taking drugs?

BLACK. Not that I know of.

WHITE. Then what is the point? I dont get it. I mean, it's hopeless. This place is just a moral leper colony.

BLACK. Damn, Professor. Moral leper colony? Where my pencil at? (*He pretends to rummage through the kitchen table drawer.*)

WHITE. Well it is.

BLACK. I aint never goin to want you to leave. Put that in my book.

WHITE. In your book?

BLACK. *In the Moral Leper Colony.* Damn, I like the sound of that.

WHITE. You're kidding me.

BLACK. You know I aint writin' no book.

WHITE. Well I still dont get it. Why not go someplace where you might be able to do some good?

BLACK. As opposed to someplace where good was needed.

WHITE. Even God gives up at some point. There's no ministry in hell. That I ever heard of.

BLACK. No there aint. That's well put. Ministry is for the livin. That's why you responsible for your brother. Once he's quit breathin you cant help him no more. After that he's in the hands of other parties. So you got to look after him now. You might even want to monitor his train schedule.

WHITE. You think you are your brother's keeper.

BLACK. I dont believe *think* quite says it.

WHITE. And Jesus is a part of this enterprise.

BLACK. Is that okay with you?

WHITE. And he's interested in coming here to this cesspool and salvaging what everybody knows is unsalvageable. Why would he do that? You said he didnt have a lot of free time. Why would he come here? What would be the difference to him between a building that was morally and spiritually vacant and one that was just plain empty?

BLACK. Mm. Professor you a theologian here and I didnt even know it.

WHITE. You're being facetious.

BLACK. I dont know that word. Dont be afraid to talk down to me. You aint goin to hurt my feelins.

WHITE. It means. I guess it means that you're not being sincere. That you dont mean what you're saying. In a cynical sort of way.

BLACK. Mm. You think I dont mean what I'm sayin.

WHITE. Sometimes. I think you say things for effect.

BLACK. Mm. Well, let me say this for effect.

WHITE. Go ahead.

BLACK. Suppose I was to tell you that if you could bring yourself to unlatch your hands from around your brother's throat you could have life everlastin?

WHITE. There's no such thing. Everybody dies.

BLACK. That aint what he said. He said you could have life everlastin. Life. Have it today. Hold it in your hand. That you could see it. It gives off a light. It's got a little weight to it. Not much. Warm to the touch. Just a little. And it's forever. And you can have it. Now. Today. But you dont want it. You dont want it cause to get it you got to let you brother off the hook. You got to actually take him and hold him in your arms and it dont make no difference what color he is or what he smells like or even if he dont want to *be* held. And the *reason* you wont do it is because he dont deserve it. And about that there aint no argument. He *dont* deserve it. *(He leans forward, slow and deliberate.)* You wont do it because it aint just. Aint that so? *(Silence.)* Aint it?

WHITE. I dont believe in those sorts of things.

BLACK. Just answer the question, Professor.

WHITE. I dont think in those terms.

BLACK. I know you dont. Answer the question.

WHITE. I suppose there's some truth in what you say.

BLACK. But that's all I'm goin to get.

WHITE. Yes.

BLACK. Well. That's all right. I'll take it. Some is a lot. We down to breadcrumbs here.

WHITE. I really have to go.

BLACK. Just stay. Just a little. We can talk bout somethin else. You like baseball? Tell you what. Why dont I fix us somethin to eat?

WHITE. I'm not hungry.

BLACK. How about some coffee then?

WHITE. All right. But then I've got to go.

BLACK. *(Rising.)* All right. The man says all right. *(He runs water in the kettle at the sink and pours the water into the percolator.)* You see I wouldnt be this rude under normal circumstances. Man come in my house and set at my table and me not offer him nothin? But with you I figure I got to strategize. Got to play my cards right. Keep you from slippin' off into the night. *(He spoons coffee from a can into the percolator and plugs the percolator in.)*

WHITE. It's not night.

BLACK. Depends on what kind of night we talkin bout. *(He comes back to the table and sits.)* Let me ask you kindly a personal question.

WHITE. This will be good.

BLACK. What do *you* think is wrong with you that has finally narrowed all your choices down to the Sunset Limited?

WHITE. I dont think there's anything wrong with me. I think I've just been driven to finally face the truth. If I'm different it doesnt mean I'm crazy.

BLACK. Different.

WHITE. Yes.

BLACK. Different from who?

WHITE. From anybody.

BLACK. What about them other folks tryin to off theyselves?

WHITE. What about them?

BLACK. Well, maybe them is the folks that you is like. Maybe them folks is your natural kin. Only you all just dont get together all that much.

WHITE. I dont think so.

BLACK. Dont think so.

WHITE. No. I've been in group therapy with those people. I never found anyone there that I felt any kinship with.

BLACK. What about them other professors? They aint no kinship there?

WHITE. *(Disgustedly.)* Good god.

BLACK. I'm goin to take that for a no.

WHITE. I loathe them and they loathe me.

BLACK. Well now wait a minute. Just cause you dont like em dont mean you *aint* like em. What was that word? Loathe?

WHITE. Loathe.

36

BLACK. That's a pretty powerful word, aint it?

WHITE. Not powerful enough, I'm afraid.

BLACK. So how come you be loathin these other professors?

WHITE. I know what you're thinking.

BLACK. What am I thinkin?

WHITE. You're thinking that I loathe them because I'm like them and I loathe myself.

BLACK. *(Sitting back in his chair.)* Damn, Professor. If I had your brains aint no tellin what all I might of done. I'd of been a drug king or somethin. Ride round in a Rolls Royce.

WHITE. You're being facetious again.

BLACK. No I aint. I wasnt the first time. Let me ask you this.

WHITE. All right.

BLACK. Is you on any kind of medication?

WHITE. No.

BLACK. They aint got no medication for pilgrims waitin to take the Sunset?

WHITE. For suicidal depression.

BLACK. Yeah.

WHITE. Yes. They do. I've tried them.

BLACK. And what happened?

WHITE. Nothing happened.

BLACK. You didnt get no relief.

WHITE. No. I think the coffee's percolated.

BLACK. I know. Does these drugs work for most folks?

WHITE. Yes. For most.

BLACK. But not for you.

WHITE. Not for me. No.

BLACK. *(Rising.)* And what do you make of that?

WHITE. I dont know. What am I supposed to make of it?

BLACK. *(Crossing to kitchen counter.)* I dont know, Professor. I just tryin to find you some constituents out there somewheres.

WHITE. Constituents?

BLACK. *(Unplugging percolator and getting down cups.)* Yeah. You like that?

WHITE. Is that a word they use on the streets?

BLACK. Naw. I learned that word in the jailhouse. You pick up stuff from these jailhouse lawyers and then it gets used around. Be talkin bout your constituents. Some other cat's constituents. Your *wife's* constituents. You use cream and sugar?

WHITE. No. Just black.

BLACK. Just black.

WHITE. Why do I have to have constituents?

BLACK. I aint said you *got* to. I just wondered if maybe you do and we just aint looked hard enough. *(He brings the percolator and the cups to the table and pours.)* They could be out there. Maybe they's some other drugproof terminal commuters out there that could be your friends.

WHITE. Terminal commuters?

BLACK. Got a nice sound to it, aint it?

WHITE. It's all right.

BLACK. *(Sitting.)* Nobody.

WHITE. Nobody. No.

BLACK. Hm.

WHITE. I'm not a member. I never wanted to be. I never was.

BLACK. Not a member.

WHITE. No.

BLACK. Well. Sometimes people dont know what they want till they get it.

WHITE. Maybe. But I think they know what they dont want.

BLACK. I dont know, Professor. I try and go by what I see. The simplest things has got more to em than you can ever understand. Bunch of people standin around on a train platform of a mornin. Waitin to go to work. Been there a hundred times. A thousand maybe. It's just a train platform. Aint nothin else much you can say about it. But they might be one commuter waitin there on the edge of that platform that for him it's somethin else. It might even be the edge of the world. The edge of the universe. He's starin at the end of all tomorrows and he's drawin a shade over ever yesterday that ever was. So he's a different kind of commuter. He's worlds away from them everday travelers. Nothin to do with them at all. Well. Is that right?

WHITE. I dont know.

BLACK. I know you dont. Bless your heart. I know you dont. *(They sip their coffee.)* You ride that subway ever day, Professor?

WHITE. Yes.

BLACK. What do you think about them people?

WHITE. On the subway?

BLACK. On the subway.

WHITE. I try not to think about them at all.

BLACK. You ever speak to any of em?

WHITE. Speak to them?

BLACK. Yeah.

WHITE. About what?

BLACK. About anything.

WHITE. No. God no.

BLACK. God no?

WHITE. Yes. God no.

BLACK. You ever curse em?

WHITE. Curse them?

BLACK. Yeah.

WHITE. Why would I do that?

BLACK. I dont know. Do you?

WHITE. No. Of course not.

BLACK. I mean where they cant hear it.

WHITE. What do you mean?

BLACK. Maybe just under your breath. In your heart. To yourself.

WHITE. Because?

BLACK. I dont know. Maybe they just in your way. Or you dont like the way they look. The way they smell. What they doin.

WHITE. And I would mutter something ugly under my breath.

BLACK. Yeah.

WHITE. I suppose.

BLACK. And how often do you reckon you might do that?

WHITE. You really dont get to interrogate me, you know.

BLACK. I know. How often?

WHITE. I dont know. With some frequency. Probably.

BLACK. Give me a number.

WHITE. A number?

BLACK. Yeah. Say just on a average day.

WHITE. I've no idea.

BLACK. Sure you do.

WHITE. A number.

BLACK. I'm a number man.

WHITE. Two or three times a day, I would guess. Something like that. Maybe.

BLACK. Could be more.

WHITE. Oh yes.

BLACK. Could be five?

WHITE. Probably.

BLACK. Ten?

WHITE. That might be a bit high.

BLACK. But we can go with five. That's safe.

WHITE. Yes.

BLACK. That's eighteen twenty-five. Can we round that off to two grand?

WHITE. What's that, per year?

BLACK. Yeah.

WHITE. Two thousand? That's a lot.

BLACK. Yes it is. But is it accurate?

WHITE. I suppose. So?

BLACK. So. I aint goin to guess your age but let me put you on the low side and say times twenty years of commutin' and now we got forty thousand curses heaped on the heads of folks you dont even know.

WHITE. So where is this going?

BLACK. I just wondered if you ever thought about that. If it might have anything to do with the shape you has managed to get yourself in.

WHITE. It's just symptomatic of the larger issue. I dont like people.

BLACK. But you wouldnt hurt them people.

WHITE. No. Of course not.

BLACK. You sure.

WHITE. Of course I'm sure. Why would I hurt them?

BLACK. I dont know. Why would you hurt yourself?

WHITE. It's not the same thing.

BLACK. You sure about that?

WHITE. I'm not them and they're not me. I think I know the difference.

BLACK. Mm.

WHITE. More mm's.

BLACK. You sure you aint hungry?

WHITE. No.

BLACK. You aint eat nothin.

WHITE. That's all right.

BLACK. I see you eyein the door. I got to strategize, you know.

WHITE. I'm really not hungry.

BLACK. Active morning like you had you aint worked up no appetite?

WHITE. No.

BLACK. I see you lookin around. Everthing in here is clean. No, dont say nothin. It's all right. *(The black pushes back his chair and rises.)* I could eat a bite and I think you could too. *(The black goes*

40

to the refrigerator and takes out some pots. He turns on the stove. He washes his hands and dries them with a towel.) You break bread with a man you have moved on to another level of friendship. I heard somewheres that that's true the world over.

WHITE. Probably.

BLACK. I like probably. Probably from you is worth a couple of damn rights anywheres else.

WHITE. Why? Because I dont believe in anything? *(The black has put the pots on the stove to warm and he brings napkins and silverware to the table and sets them out. He sits down.)*

BLACK. Well. I dont think that's the problem. I think it's what you do believe that is carryin you off, not what you dont. Let me ask you this.

WHITE. Go ahead.

BLACK. You ever think about Jesus?

WHITE. Here we go.

BLACK. Do you?

WHITE. What makes you think I'm not jewish?

BLACK. What, Jews aint allowed to think about Jesus?

WHITE. No, but they might think about him differently.

BLACK. Is you jewish?

WHITE. No. As it happens. I'm not.

BLACK. Whew. You had me worried there for a minute.

WHITE. What, you dont like jews?

BLACK. *(Shaking his head, almost laughing.)* Pullin your chain, Professor. Pullin your chain. I dont know why I love to mess with you. But I do. You need to listen. Or you need to believe what you hearin. The whole point of where this is goin — which you wanted to know — is that they aint no jews. Aint no whites. Aint no niggers. People of color. Aint none of that. At the deep bottom of the mine where the gold is at there aint none of that. There's just the pure ore. That forever thing. That you dont think is there. That thing that helps to keep folks nailed down to the platform when the Sunset Limited comes through. Even when they think they might want to get aboard. That thing that makes it possible to ladle out benedictions upon the heads of strangers instead of curses. It's all the same thing. And it aint but one thing. Just one.

WHITE. And that would be Jesus.

BLACK. Got to think about how to answer that. Maybe one more heresy wont hurt you. You pretty loaded up on em already. Here's what I would say, I would say that the thing we are talkin' about is

41

Jesus, but it is Jesus understood as that gold at the bottom of the mine. He couldnt come down here and take the form of a man if that form was not done shaped to accommodate him. And if I said that there aint no way for Jesus to be ever man without ever man bein Jesus then I believe that might be a pretty big heresy. But that's all right. It aint as big a heresy as sayin that a man aint all that much different from a rock. Which is how your view looks to me.

WHITE. It's not my view. I believe in the primacy of the intellect.

BLACK. What is that word.

WHITE. Primacy? It means first. It means what you put first.

BLACK. And that would be intellect.

WHITE. Yes.

BLACK. What about the primacy of the Sunset Limited?

WHITE. Yes. That too.

BLACK. But not the primacy of all them folks waitin on a later train.

WHITE. No. No primacy there.

BLACK. Mm.

WHITE. Mm what.

BLACK. You tough, Professor. You tough. *(The black rises and goes to the stove. He reaches down plates and stirs the pots and ladles out the dinner He takes down a loaf of white bread and puts four slices on a plate and brings the plate of bread to the table and sets it down.)* Yeah you tough. *(The black brings the two plates to the table and sets them out and takes his seat. He looks at the professor.)* You see yourself as a questioner, Professor. But about that I got my doubts. Even so, the quest of your life is *your* quest. You on a road that *you* laid. And that fact alone might be all the reason you need for keepin to it. As long as you on that road you cant be lost.

WHITE. I'm not sure I understand what you're saying.

BLACK. Well, Professor. I have got some very serious doubts about you not understandin anything I say. Now I'm goin to say Grace. *(The black puts his hands on the table at either side of his plate and bows his head.)* Lord we thank you for this food and we ask that you keep us ever mindful of the many blessins we have received from your hand. We thank you today for the life of the professor that you have returned to us and we ask that you continue to look after him because we need him. *(Pause.)* I aint sure why we need him. I just know we do. Amen. *(The black looks up. He smiles at the professor.)* All right. You tell me if you like this.

WHITE. It looks good. *(They begin to eat.)* This is good. *(They eat.)* This is very good.

BLACK. Supposed to be good. This is soul food, my man.

WHITE. It's got what in it? Molasses?

BLACK. Mm. You a chef, Professor?

WHITE. Not really.

BLACK. But some.

WHITE. Some, yes. Bananas, of course. Mangos?

BLACK. Got a mango or two in there. Rutabagas.

WHITE. Rutabagas?

BLACK. Rutabagas. *Them* aint easy to find.

WHITE. It's very good.

BLACK. It gets better after a day or two. I just fixed this last night. You need to warm it up a few times to get the flavors right.

WHITE. Like chile.

BLACK. Like chile. That's right. You know where I learned to fix this?

WHITE. In Louisana?

BLACK. Right here in the ghettos of New York City. They's a lot of influences in a dish like this. You got many parts of the world in that pot yonder. Different countries. Different people.

WHITE. Any white people?

BLACK. Not if you can help it.

WHITE. Really?

BLACK. Messin with you, Professor. Messin with you. You know these French chefs in these uptown restaurants?

WHITE. Not personally.

BLACK. You know what they like to cook?

WHITE. No.

BLACK. Sweetbreads. Tripe. Brains. All that shit they dont nobody eat. You know why that is?

WHITE. Because it's a challenge? You have to innovate?

BLACK. You pretty smart for a cracker. A challenge. That's right. The stuff they cook is dead cheap. Most folks throws it out. Give it to the cat. But poor folks dont throw nothin out.

WHITE. I guess that's right.

BLACK. It dont take a lot of skill to make a porterhouse steak taste good. But what if you cant buy no porterhouse steak? You still wants to eat somethin that tastes good. What you do then?

WHITE. Innovate.

BLACK. Innovate. That's right, Professor. And when do you innovate?

43

WHITE. When you dont have something that you want.

BLACK. You fixin to get a A plus. So who would that be? That aint got what they want?

WHITE. Poor people.

BLACK. I love this man. So how you like this?

WHITE. It's very good.

BLACK. Well let me have your plate.

WHITE. Just a small portion.

BLACK. That's all right, Professor. You need to eat. You done had yourself a pretty busy day. *(The black puts more of the dish on the professors plate and comes to the table and sets it in front of him.)* You want some more coffee?

WHITE. Yes. That would be great. *(The black brings the pot to the table and pours his cup and sets the pot on the table and takes his seat and they continue to eat.)* You dont think a glass of wine would have been good with this?

BLACK. Oh no. I think it might of been good.

WHITE. But you wouldnt drink it.

BLACK. Oh I might. One glass.

WHITE. Jesus drank wine. He and his disciples.

BLACK. Yes he did. Accordin to the Bible. Of course it dont say nothin about him hidin it in the toilet.

WHITE. Is that really a favorite hiding place?

BLACK. Oh yes. I've knowed drunks to lift the tops off of toilet tanks in strange places just on the off chance.

WHITE. Is that true?

BLACK. Naw. It could be, though. Wouldnt surprise me none.

WHITE. What is the worst thing you ever did.

BLACK. More jailhouse stories.

WHITE. Why not?

BLACK. Which why not you want to hear?

WHITE. Is bludgeoning the man in the prison cafeteria the worst thing you ever did?

BLACK. No. It aint.

WHITE. Really? What's the worst?

BLACK. Aint goin tell you.

WHITE. Why not?

BLACK. Cause you'd jump up and run out the door hollerin.

WHITE. It must be pretty bad.

BLACK. It is pretty bad. That's why I aint tellin you.

WHITE. Now I'm afraid to ask.

BLACK. No you aint.

WHITE. Have you ever told anyone?

BLACK. Oh yeah. It wouldnt leave me alone. The soul might be silent but the servant of the soul has always got a voice and it has got one for a reason. The life of the master depends on the servant and this is one master that has got to be sustained. Got to be sustained.

WHITE. Who did you tell it to?

BLACK. I told it to a man of God who was my friend.

WHITE. What did he say?

BLACK. He didnt say a word.

WHITE. But you're not curious about the worst thing I ever did.

BLACK. Yeah I am.

WHITE. But you wont ask me what it is.

BLACK. Dont have to.

WHITE. Why is that?

BLACK. Cause I was there and I seen it.

WHITE. Well, I might have a different view.

BLACK. Yeah. You might. You want some more?

WHITE. No. I'm stuffed.

BLACK. Hungrier than you thought.

WHITE. Yes. I was.

BLACK. Good.

WHITE. Is this some kind of a test of your faith?

BLACK. What, you?

WHITE. Me. Yes.

BLACK. Naw, Professor. It aint my faith you testin.

WHITE. You see everything in black and white.

BLACK. It is black and white.

WHITE. I suppose that makes the world easier to understand.

BLACK. You might be surprised about how little time I spend trying to understand the world.

WHITE. You try to understand God.

BLACK. No I dont. I just try and understand what he wants from me.

WHITE. And that is everything you need.

BLACK. If God aint everthing you need you in a world of trouble. And if what you sayin is that my view of the world is a narrow one I dont disagree with that. Of course I could point out that I aint down on the platform in my leapin' costume.

WHITE. You could.

BLACK. A lot of things is beyond my understandin. I know that.

I say it again. If it aint in this book then they's a good chance that I dont know it. Before I started readin the Bible I was pretty much in that primacy thing myself.

WHITE. Primacy thing.

BLACK. Yeah. Not as bad as you. But pretty bad. I was pretty dumb, but I wasnt dumb enough to believe that what had got me nowheres in forty years was all of a sudden goin to get me somewheres. I was dumb, but I wasnt that dumb. I seen what was there for the askin, and I decided to ask. And that's all I done. And it was hard. I'll tell you right now, Professor, it was hard. I was layin there all cut up and chained to that hospital bed and I was cryin I hurt so bad and I thought they'd kill me if I did live and I tried to say it and tried to say it and after a while I just quit. I put all of that away from me. And I just said it. I said: Please help me. And he did. *(They sit.)*

BLACK. Long silence.

WHITE. Its just a silence.

BLACK. Well. That's my story, Professor. It's easy told. I dont make a move without Jesus. When I get up in the mornin I just try to get ahold of his belt. Oh, ever once in a while I'll catch myself slippin into manual override. But I catch myself. I catch myself.

WHITE. Manual override?

BLACK. You like that?

WHITE. It's okay.

BLACK. I thought it was pretty good.

WHITE. So you come to the end of your rope and you admit defeat and you are in despair and in this state you seize upon this whatever it is that has neither substance nor sense and you grab hold of it and hang on for dear life. Is that a fair portrayal?

BLACK. Well, that could be one way to say it.

WHITE. It doesnt make any sense.

BLACK. Well, I thought when we was talkin earlier I heard you to say they wasnt none of it made no sense. Talkin bout the history of the world and all such as that.

WHITE. It doesnt. On a larger scale. But what you're telling me isnt a view of things. Its a view of one thing. And I find it nonsensical.

BLACK. What would you do if Jesus was to speak to you?

WHITE. Why? Do you imagine that he might?

BLACK. No. I dont. But I dont know.

WHITE. I'm not virtuous enough.

BLACK. No, Professor, it aint nothin like that. You dont have to

46

be virtuous. You just has to be quiet. I cant speak for the Lord but the experience I've had leads me to believe that he'll speak to anybody that'll listen. You damn sure aint got to be virtuous.

WHITE. Well if I heard God talking to me, then I'd be ready for you to take me up to Bellevue. As you suggested.

BLACK. What if what he said made sense?

WHITE. It wouldnt make any difference. Craziness is craziness.

BLACK. Dont make no difference if it makes sense.

WHITE. No.

BLACK. Mm. Well, that's about as bad a case of the primacy as I ever heard.

WHITE. Well. I've always gone my own way. *Ich kann nicht anders.*

BLACK. What is that you talkin?

WHITE. It's German

BLACK. You talk German?

WHITE. Not really. A little. It's a quotation.

BLACK. Didnt do them Germans much good though, did it?

WHITE. I dont know. The Germans contributed a great deal to civilization. *(Pause.)* Before Hitler.

BLACK. And then they contributed Hitler.

WHITE. If you like.

BLACK. Wasnt none of my doin.

WHITE. I gather it to be your belief that culture tends to contribute to human misery. That the more one knows the more unhappy one is likely to be.

BLACK. As in the case of certain parties known to us.

WHITE. As in the case.

BLACK. I dont believe I said that. In fact, I think maybe you said it.

WHITE. I never said it.

BLACK. Mm. But do you believe it?

WHITE. No.

BLACK. No?

WHITE. I dont know. It could be true.

BLACK. Well why is that? It dont seem right, does it?

WHITE. It's the first thing in that book there. The Garden of Eden. Knowledge as destructive to the spirit. Destructive to goodness.

BLACK. I thought you aint read this book.

WHITE. Everyone knows that story. It's probably the most famous story in there.

BLACK. So why do you think that is?

WHITE. I suppose from the God point of view all knowledge is

47

vanity. Or maybe it gives people the unhealthy illusion that they can outwit the devil.

BLACK. Damn, Professor. Where was you when I needed you?

WHITE. You'd better be careful.You see where it's gotten me.

BLACK. I do see. It's the subject at hand.

WHITE. The darker picture is always the correct one. When you read the history of the world you are reading a saga of bloodshed and greed and folly the import of which is impossible to ignore. And yet we imagine that the future will somehow be different. I've no idea why we are even still here but in all probability we will not be here much longer.

BLACK. Them is some pretty powerful words, Professor. That's what's in your heart, aint it?

WHITE. Yes.

BLACK. Well I can relate to them thoughts.

WHITE. You can?

BLACK. Yes I can.

WHITE. That surprises me. What, you're going to think about them?

BLACK. I done have thought about em. I've thought about em for a long time. Not as good as you said it. But pretty close.

WHITE. Well you surprise me. And you've come to what conclusions?

BLACK. I aint. I'm still thinkin.

WHITE. Yes. Well, I'm not.

BLACK. Things can change.

WHITE. No they cant.

BLACK. You could be wrong.

WHITE. I dont think so.

BLACK. But that aint somethin you have a lot of in your life.

WHITE. What isnt?

BLACK. Bein wrong.

WHITE. I admit it when I'm wrong.

BLACK. I dont think so.

WHITE. Well, you're entitled to your opinion. *(The black leans back and regards the professor. He reaches and picks up the newspaper from the table and leans back again and adjusts his glasses.)*

BLACK. Let's see here. Story on page three. *(He folds the paper elaborately.)* Yeah. Here it is. Friends report that the man had ignored all advice and had stated that he intended to pursue his own course. *(He adjusts his glasses.)* A close confidant stated *(He looks up.)* — and this here is a quotation — said: You couldnt tell the son of a bitch nothin. *(He looks up again.)* Can you say that in the papers? Son of a bitch? Meanwhile, bloodspattered spectators at the hundred and fifty-fifth street station — continued on page four. *(He wets his thumb and laboriously turns the page and refolds the paper.)* — who were interviewed at the scene all reported that the man's last words as he hurtled toward the oncomin commuter train were: I am right. *(He lays down the paper and adjusts his spectacles and peers over the top of them at the professor.)*

WHITE. Very funny. *(The black takes off his glasses and lowers his head and pinches the bridge of his nose and shakes his head.)*

BLACK. Oh Professor. Mm. You an amazin man.

WHITE. I'm glad you find me entertaining.

BLACK. Well, you pretty special.

WHITE. I dont think I'm special.

BLACK. You dont.

WHITE. No. I dont.

BLACK. You dont think you might view them other commuters from a certain height?

WHITE. I view those other commuters as fellow occupants of the same abyssal pit in which I find myself. If they see it as something else I dont know how that makes me special.

BLACK. Mm. I hear what you sayin. But still I keep comin back to them commuters. Them that's waitin on the Sunset? I got to think maybe they could be just a little bit special theyselves. I mean, they got to be in a deeper pit than just us daytravelers. A deeper and a darker. I aint sayin they down as deep as you, but pretty deep maybe.

WHITE. So?

BLACK. So how come they cant be your brothers in despair and self-destruction? I thought misery loved company?

WHITE. I'm sure I dont know.

BLACK. Well let me take a shot at it.

WHITE. Be my guest.

BLACK. What I think is that you got better reasons then them. I mean, their reasons is just that they dont like it here, but yours says what they is not to like and why not to like it. You got more intelligent reasons. More elegant reasons.

WHITE. Are you making fun of me?

BLACK. No. I aint.

WHITE. But you think I'm full of shit.

49

BLACK. I dont think that. Oh I dont doubt but what it's possible to die from bein full of shit. But I dont think that's what we lookin at here.

WHITE. What do you think we're looking at?

BLACK. I dont know. You got me on unfamiliar ground. You got these elegant world class reasons for takin the Limited and these other dudes all they got is maybe they just dont feel good. In fact, it might could be that you aint even all that unhappy.

WHITE. You think that my education is driving me to suicide.

BLACK. Well, no. I'm just posin the question. Wait a minute. Fore you answer. *(He takes his pad and his pencil and begins to write laboriously, his tongue in the corner of his mouth, grimacing. This for the professor's benefit. He looks sideways at him and smiles. He tears off the page and folds it and puts it in his shirtpocket.)* All right. Go ahead.

WHITE. I think that's the most ridiculous thing I ever heard. *(The black takes the folded paper from his pocket and hands it across. The professor opens it and reads it aloud.)* I think that's the most ridiculous thing I ever heard. Very clever. What's the point?

BLACK. The point dont change. The point is always the same point. It's what I said before and what I keep lookin for ways to say it again. The light is all around you, cept you dont see nothin but shadow. And the shadow is you. You the one makin it.

WHITE. Well, I dont have your faith. Why dont we just leave it at that.

BLACK. You dont never think about maybe just startin over?

WHITE. I did. At one time. I dont any more.

BLACK. Sometimes faith might just be a case of not havin nothin else left.

WHITE. Well, I do have something else.

BLACK. Maybe you could just keep that in reserve. Maybe just take a shot at startin over. I dont mean start again. Everbody's done that. Over means over. It means you just walk away. I mean, if everthing you are and everthing you have and everthing you have done has brought you at last to the bottom of a whiskey bottle or bought you a one way ticket on the Sunset Limited then you cant give me the first reason on God's earth for salvagin none of it. Cause they aint no reason. And I'm goin to tell you that if you can bring yourself to shut the door on all of that it will be cold and it will be lonely and they'll be a mean wind blowin. And them is all good signs. You dont say nothin. You just turn up your collar and keep walkin.

WHITE. I cant.

50

BLACK. Yeah.

WHITE. I cant.

BLACK. You want some more coffee?

WHITE. No. Thank you.

BLACK. Why do you think folks takes their own lives?

WHITE. I dont know. Different reasons.

BLACK. Yeah. But is there somethin them different reasons has got in common?

WHITE. I cant speak for others. My own reasons center around a gradual loss of make-believe. That's all. A gradual enlightenment as to the nature of reality. Of the world.

BLACK. Them worldly reasons.

WHITE. If you like.

BLACK. Them elegant reasons.

WHITE. That was your description.

BLACK. You didnt disagree with it. *(The professor shrugs.)* It's them reasons that your brother dont know nothin about hangin by his necktie from the steampipe down in the basement. He got his own dumb-ass reasons, but maybe if we could educate him to where some of them more elegant reasons was available to him and his buddies then they'd be a lot of folks out there could off theyselves with more joy in they hearts. What do you think?

WHITE. Now I know you're being facetious.

BLACK. This time I think you're right. I think you have finally drove me to it.

WHITE. Mm hm.

BLACK. Well, the professor's done gone to layin the mm hm's on me. I better watch my step.

WHITE. Yes you had. I might be warming up the trick bag.

BLACK. But still you think that your reasons is about the world and his is mostly just about him.

WHITE. I think that's probably true.

BLACK. I see a different truth. Settin right across the table from me.

WHITE. Which is?

BLACK. That you must love your brother or die.

WHITE. I dont know what that means. That's another world from anything I know.

BLACK. What's the world you know.

WHITE. You dont want to hear.

BLACK. Sure I do.

WHITE. I dont think so.

51

BLACK. Go ahead.

WHITE. All right. It's that the world is basically a forced labor camp from which the workers — perfectly innocent — are led forth by lottery, a few each day, to be executed. I dont think that this is just the way I see it. I think it's the way it is. Are there alternate views? Of course. Will any of them stand close scrutiny? No.

BLACK. Man.

WHITE. So. Do you want to take a look at that train schedule again?

BLACK. And they aint nothin to be done about it.

WHITE. No. The efforts that people undertake to improve the world invariably make it worse. I used to think there were exceptions to that dictum. I dont think that now. *(The black sits back, looking down at the table. He shakes his head slightly.)* What else do you want to talk about?

BLACK. I dont know. Them sounds to me like the words of a man on his way to the train station.

WHITE. They are those words.

BLACK. What do you think about that man?

WHITE. I'm like you. I dont. I used to. Now I dont. I think about minimalizing pain. That is my life. I dont know why it isnt everyone's.

BLACK. You dont think gettin' run over by a train might smart just a little?

WHITE. No. I did the calculations. At seventy miles an hour the train is outrunning the neurons. It should be totally painless.

BLACK. I'm goin to be stuck with your ass for a while, aint I?

WHITE. I hope not

BLACK. If this aint the life you had in mind, what was?

WHITE. I dont know. Not this. Is your life the one you'd planned?

BLACK. No, it aint. I got what I needed instead of what I wanted and that's just about the best kind of luck you can have.

WHITE. Yes. Well.

BLACK. You cant compare your life to mine, can you?

WHITE. In all honesty, no. I cant.

BLACK. Mm.

WHITE. I'm sorry. I should go.

BLACK. You dont have to go.

WHITE. I've offended you.

BLACK. I got a thicker hide than that, Professor. Just stay. You aint hurt my feelins.

WHITE. I know you think that I should be thankful and I'm sorry not to be.

BLACK. Now Professor, I dont think no such a thing.

WHITE. I should go.

BLACK. I'm diggin a dry hole here, aint I?

WHITE. I admire your persistence.

BLACK. What can I do to get you to stay a bit?

WHITE. Why? Are you hoping that if I stay long enough God might speak to me?

BLACK. No, I'm hopin' he might speak to me.

WHITE. I know you think I at least owe you a little more of my time. I know I'm ungrateful. But ingratitude is not the sin to a spiritual bankrupt that it is to a man of God.

BLACK. You dont owe me nothin, Professor.

WHITE. Do you really think that?

BLACK. Yes. I really do.

WHITE. Well. You're very kind. I wish there was something I could do to repay you but there isnt. So why dont we just say goodbye and you can get on with your life.

BLACK. I cant.

WHITE. You cant?

BLACK. No.

WHITE. What do you want me to do?

BLACK. I dont know. Suppose you could wake up tomorrow and you wouldnt be wantin' to jump in front of no train. Suppose all you had to do was ask. Would you do it?

WHITE. It would depend on what I had to give up.

BLACK. I started to write that down and put it in my pocket.

WHITE. What is it that you think I'm holding on to? What is it that the terminal commuter cherishes that he would die for?

BLACK. I dont know. I dont know.

WHITE. No.

BLACK. You dont want to talk to me no more, do you?

WHITE. I thought you had a thick skin.

BLACK. It's pretty thick. It aint hide to the bone.

WHITE. *Why* do you think it? Why do you think there is something?

BLACK. I dont know. It just seems to me that a man that cant wait for a train to run over him has got to have *somethin* on his mind. Most folks would settle for maybe just a slap up the side of the head. You say you dont care about nothin but I dont believe that. I dont believe that death is ever about nothin. You asked me what I thought it was you was holdin on to and I got to say I dont know. Or maybe I just dont have the words to say it. And maybe you know but you aint sayin. But I believe that when you took your celebrated leap you was holdin on to it and takin it with you. Holdin on for grim death. I look for the words, Professor. I look for the words because I believe that the words is the way to your heart.

WHITE. You think that anyone in my position is automatically blind to the workings of his own psyche.

BLACK. I think that anybody in your position is automatically blind. But that aint the whole story. Because we still talkin bout the rest of them third railers and them takin one train and you takin another.

WHITE. I didnt say that.

BLACK. Sure you did. They got a train for all them dumb-ass crackers that just feels bad and then they got this other train for you cause your pain and the world's pain is the same pain and this train requires a observation car and a diner.

WHITE. Well. You can think what you want. You dont need my agreement.

BLACK. I know. But that aint the way to the trick bag.

WHITE. Well. The trick bag seems to have shaped itself up into some sort of communal misery wherein one finds salvation by consorting among the loathsome.

BLACK. Damn, Professor. You puttin me in the bag. Where you come up with stuff like that?

WHITE. It was phrased especially for you. For your enjoyment. You see what a whore I am?

BLACK. No you aint. You a smart man. Too smart for me.

WHITE. I feel the bag yawning.

BLACK. I wish I knew how.

WHITE. Do you really think that? That I'm too smart for you?

BLACK. Yes I do. If you can jack you own self around nine ways from Sunday I'd like to know what chance you think I got.

WHITE. I see.

BLACK. What I need to do here is to buy more time. But I dont know what to buy it with.

WHITE. You dont know what to offer a man about to board the Limited.

BLACK. No. I dont. I feel like I'm about traded out.

WHITE. Maybe you are. Have you ever dealt with suicides?

54

BLACK. No. You the first one. These junkies and crackheads is about as far from suicide as you can get. They wouldnt even know what you was talkin' about. They wake up in pain ever day. Bad pain. But they aint headed for the depot. Now you can say, well, they got a fix for their pain. Just need to hustle on out there and get it. And that's a good argument. But still we got this question. Just what is this pain that is causin these express riders to belly up at the kiosk with the black crepe. What kind of pain we talkin about? I got to say that if it was grief that brought folks to suicide it'd be a full time job just to get em all in the ground come sundown. So I keep comin back to the same question. If it aint what you lost that is more than you can bear then maybe it's what you wont lose. What you'd rather die than to give up.

WHITE. But if you die you will give it up.

BLACK. No you wont. You wont be here.

WHITE. Well. I cant help you. Letting it all go is the place I finally got to. It took a lot of work to get there and if there is one thing I would be unwilling to give up it is exactly that.

BLACK. You got any other way of sayin that?

WHITE. The one thing I wont give up is giving up. I expect that to carry me through. I'm depending on it. The things I believed in were very frail. As I said. They wont be around for long and neither will I. But I dont think that's really the reason for my decision. I think it goes deeper. You can acclimate yourself to loss. You have to. I mean, you like music, right?

BLACK. Yes I do.

WHITE. Who's the greatest composer you know of?

BLACK. John Coltrane. Hands down.

WHITE. Do you think his music will last forever?

BLACK. Well. Forever's a long time, Professor. So I got to say no. It wont.

WHITE. But that doesnt make it worthless, does it?

BLACK. No it dont.

WHITE. You give up the world line by line. Stoically. And then one day you realize that your courage is farcical. It doesnt mean anything. You've become an accomplice in your own annihilation and there is nothing you can do about it. Everything you do closes a door somewhere ahead of you. And finally there is only one door left.

BLACK. That's a dark world, Professor.

WHITE. Yes.

BLACK. What's the worst thing ever happen to you?

WHITE. Getting snatched off a subway platform one morning by an emissary of Jesus.

BLACK. I'm serious.

WHITE. So am I.

BLACK. Before this mornin. What was the worst thing.

WHITE. I dont know.

BLACK. Well, let's pretend you dont know then. Still, do you reckon it was about you? Or about somebody close to you?

WHITE. Probably someone close to me.

BLACK. I think that's probably right. Dont that tell you somethin?

WHITE. Yes. Dont get close to people.

BLACK. You a hard case, man.

WHITE. How else could I win your love?

BLACK. You probably right. Let me try this. I dont believe that the world can be better than what you allow it to be. Dark a world as you live in, they aint goin to be a whole lot of surprises in the way of good news.

WHITE. I'm sure that's true.

BLACK. Well jubilation. Listen at the professor.

WHITE. But I'm at a loss as to how to bring myself to believe in some most excellent world when I already know that it doesnt exist.

BLACK. Most excellent.

WHITE. Yes.

BLACK. I sure do like that. Most excellent.

WHITE. Do you actually believe in such a world?

BLACK. Yes I do, Professor. Yes I do. I think it's there for the askin. You got to get in the right line. Buy the right ticket. Take that regular commuter train and stay off the express. Stay on the platform with your fellow commuter. You might even want to nod at him. Maybe even say hello. All of them is travelers too. And they's some of em been places that most people dont want to go to. They didnt neither. They might even tell you how they got there and maybe save you a trip you'll be thankful you didnt take.

WHITE. Yes. Well, that's not going to happen.

BLACK. Why not?

WHITE. Because I dont believe in that world. I just want to take the train. Look, why dont I just go?

BLACK. How about some more coffee?

WHITE. No thank you.

BLACK. What can I do?

WHITE. Maybe you just need to accept that you're in over your head.

BLACK. I do accept it. It dont let me off the hook though.

WHITE. You think I dont understand. But I'm not sure you'd want to listen to the things I do understand.

BLACK. Try me.

WHITE. It would just upset you.

BLACK. I been upset before.

WHITE. It's worse than you think.

BLACK. That's all right.

WHITE. You dont want to hear this.

BLACK. Yes I do. I got no choice. *(The professor leans back and studies the black.)*

WHITE. Okay. Maybe you're right. Well, here's my news, Reverend. I yearn for the darkness. I pray for death. Real death. If I thought that in death I would meet the people I've known in life I dont know what I'd do. That would be the ultimate horror. The ultimate despair. If I had to meet my mother again and start all of that all over, only this time without the prospect of death to look forward to? Well. That would be the final nightmare. Kafka on wheels.

BLACK. Damn, Professor. You dont want to see you own mama?

WHITE. No. I dont. I told you this would upset you. I want the dead to be dead. Forever. And I want to be one of them. Except that of course you cant be one of them. You cant be one of the dead because what has no existence can have no community. No community. My heart warms just thinking about it. Silence. Blackness. Aloneness. Peace. And all of it only a heartbeat away.

BLACK. Damn, Professor.

WHITE. Let me finish. I dont regard my state of mind as some pessimistic view of the world. I regard it as the world itself. Evolution cannot avoid bringing intelligent life ultimately to an awareness of one thing above all else and that one thing is futility.

BLACK. Mm. If I'm understandin you right you sayin that everbody that aint just eat up with the dumb-ass ought to be suicidal.

WHITE. Yes.

BLACK. You aint shittin me?

WHITE. No. I'm not shitting you. If people saw the world for what it truly is. Saw their lives for what they truly are. Without dreams or illusions. I dont believe they could offer the first reason why they should not elect to die as soon as possible.

BLACK. Damn, Professor.

WHITE. *(Coldly.)* I dont believe in God. Can you understand that? Look around you man. Cant you see? The clamor and din of those in torment has to be the sound most pleasing to his ear. And I loathe these discussions. The argument of the village atheist whose single passion is to revile endlessly that which he denies the existence of in the first place. Your fellowship is a fellowship of pain and nothing more. And if that pain were actually collective instead of simply reiterative then the sheer weight of it would drag the world from the walls of the universe and send it crashing and burning through whatever night it might yet be capable of engendering until it was not even ash. And justice? Brotherhood? Eternal life? Good god, man. Show me a religion that prepares one for death. For nothingness. There's a church I might enter. Yours prepares one only for more life. For dreams and illusions and lies. If you could banish the fear of death from men's hearts they wouldnt live a day. Who would want this nightmare if not for fear of the next? The shadow of the axe hangs over every joy. Every road ends in death. Or worse. Every friendship. Every love. Torment, betrayal, loss, suffering, pain, age, indignity, and hideous lingering illness. All with a single conclusion. For you and for every one and every thing that you have chosen to care for. There's the true brotherhood. The true fellowship. And everyone is a member for life. You tell me that my brother is my salvation? My salvation? Well then damn him. Damn him in every shape and form and guise. Do I see myself in him? Yes. I do. And what I see sickens me. Do you understand me? *Can* you understand me? *(The black sits with his head lowered.)* I'm sorry.

BLACK. That's all right.

WHITE. No. I'm sorry. *(The black looks up at him.)*

BLACK. How long you felt like this?

WHITE. All my life.

BLACK. And that's the truth.

WHITE. It's worse than that.

BLACK. I dont see what could be worse than that.

WHITE. Rage is really only for the good days. The truth is there's little of that left. The truth is that the forms I see have been slowly emptied out. They no longer have any content. They are shapes only. A train, a wall, a world. Or a man. A thing dangling in senseless articulation in a howling void. No meaning to its life. Its words. Why would I seek the company of such a thing? Why?

BLACK. Damn.

WHITE. You see what it is you've saved.

BLACK. Tried to save. Am tryin. Tryin hard.

WHITE. Yes.

BLACK. Who is my brother.

WHITE. Your brother.

BLACK. Yes.

WHITE. Is that why I'm here? In your apartment?

BLACK. No. But it's why I am.

WHITE. You asked what I was a professor of. I'm a professor of darkness. The night in day's clothing. And now I wish you all the very best but I must go. *(He pushes back his chair and rises.)*

BLACK. Just stay a few more minutes.

WHITE. No. No more time. Goodbye. *(He turns toward the door and the black rises.)*

BLACK. Come on, Professor. We can talk about somethin else. I promise.

WHITE. I dont want to talk about something else.

BLACK. Dont go out there. You know what's out there.

WHITE. Oh yes. Indeed I do. I know what is out there and I know who is out there. I rush to nuzzle his bony cheek. No doubt he'll be surprised to find himself so cherished. And as I cling to his neck I will whisper in that dry and ancient ear: Here I am. Here I am. Now open the door.

BLACK. Dont do it, Professor.

WHITE. I'm sorry. You're a kind man, but I have to go. I've heard you out and you've heard me and there's no more to say. Your God must have once stood in a dawn of infinite possibility and this is what he's made of it. And now it is drawing to a close. You say that I want God's love. I dont. Perhaps I want forgiveness, but there is no one to ask it of. And there is no going back. No setting things right. Perhaps once. Not now. Now there is only the hope of nothingness. I cling to that hope. Now open the door. Please.

BLACK. Dont do it.

WHITE. Open the door. *(The black undoes the chains. They rattle to the floor. He opens the door and the professor exits. The black stands in the doorway looking down the hall.)*

BLACK. Professor? I know you dont mean them words. Professor? I'm goin to be there in the mornin. I'll be there. You hear? I'll be there in the mornin. *(He collapses to his knees in the doorway, all but weeping.)* I'll be there. *(He looks up.)* He didnt mean them words. You know he didnt. You know he didnt. I dont understand what you sent me down there for. I dont understand it. If you wanted me to help him how come you didnt give me the words? You give em to him. What about me? *(He kneels weeping rocking back and forth.)* That's all right. That's all right. If you never speak again you know I'll keep your word. You know I will. You know I'm good for it. *(He lifts his head.)* Is that okay? Is that okay?

End of Play

PROPERTY LIST

Bible
Pad and Pencil
Kettle
Percolator
Coffee in can
2 cups
Pots
Kitchen table with drawer
Stove
Dish towel
Napkins
Silverware
Ladle
Load of white bread
2 plates
Newspaper
Eyeglasses
Chains on door

NEW PLAYS

★ **A CIVIL WAR CHRISTMAS: AN AMERICAN MUSICAL CELEBRA-TION by Paula Vogel, music by Daryl Waters.** It's 1864, and Washington, D.C. is settling down to the coldest Christmas Eve in years. Intertwining many lives, this musical shows us that the gladness of one's heart is the best gift of all. "Boldly inventive theater, warm and affecting." *–Talkin' Broadway.* "Crisp strokes of dialogue." *–NY Times.* [12M, 5W] ISBN: 978-0-8222-2361-0

★ **SPEECH & DEBATE by Stephen Karam.** Three teenage misfits in Salem, Oregon discover they are linked by a sex scandal that's rocked their town. "Savvy comedy." *–Variety.* "Hilarious, cliché-free, and immensely entertaining." *–NY Times.* "A strong, rangy play." *–NY Newsday.* [2M, 2W] ISBN: 978-0-8222-2286-6

★ **DIVIDING THE ESTATE by Horton Foote.** Matriarch Stella Gordon is determined not to divide her 100-year-old Texas estate, despite her family's declining wealth and the looming financial crisis. But her three children have another plan. "Goes for laughs and succeeds." *–NY Daily News.* "The theatrical equivalent of a page-turner." *–Bloomberg.com.* [4M, 9W] ISBN: 978-0-8222-2398-6

★ **WHY TORTURE IS WRONG, AND THE PEOPLE WHO LOVE THEM by Christopher Durang.** Christopher Durang turns political humor upside down with this raucous and provocative satire about America's growing homeland "insecurity." "A smashing new play." *–NY Observer.* "You may laugh yourself silly." *–Bloomberg News.* [4M, 3W] ISBN: 978-0-8222-2401-3

★ **FIFTY WORDS by Michael Weller.** While their nine-year-old son is away for the night on his first sleepover, Adam and Jan have an evening alone together, beginning a suspenseful nightlong roller-coaster ride of revelation, rancor, passion and humor. "Mr. Weller is a bold and productive dramatist." *–NY Times.* [1M, 1W] ISBN: 978-0-8222-2348-1

★ **BECKY'S NEW CAR by Steven Dietz.** Becky Foster is caught in middle age, middle management and in a middling marriage—with no prospects for change on the horizon. Then one night a socially inept and grief-struck millionaire stumbles into the car dealership where Becky works. "Gently and consistently funny." *–Variety.* "Perfect blend of hilarious comedy and substantial weight." *–Broadway Hour.* [4M, 3W] ISBN: 978-0-8222-2393-1

DRAMATISTS PLAY SERVICE, INC.
440 Park Avenue South, New York, NY 10016 212-683-8960 Fax 212-213-1539
postmaster@dramatists.com www.dramatists.com

NEW PLAYS

★ **AT HOME AT THE ZOO by Edward Albee.** Edward Albee delves deeper into his play THE ZOO STORY by adding a first act, HOMELIFE, which precedes Peter's fateful meeting with Jerry on a park bench in Central Park. "An essential and heartening experience." *–NY Times.* "Darkly comic and thrilling." *–Time Out.* "Genuinely fascinating." *–Journal News.* [2M, 1W] ISBN: 978-0-8222-2317-7

★ **PASSING STRANGE book and lyrics by Stew, music by Stew and Heidi Rodewald, created in collaboration with Annie Dorsen.** A daring musical about a young bohemian that takes you from black middle-class America to Amsterdam, Berlin and beyond on a journey towards personal and artistic authenticity. "Fresh, exuberant, bracingly inventive, bitingly funny, and full of heart." *–NY Times.* "The freshest musical in town!" *–Wall Street Journal.* "Excellent songs and a vulnerable heart." *–Variety.* [4M, 3W] ISBN: 978-0-8222-2400-6

★ **REASONS TO BE PRETTY by Neil LaBute.** Greg really, truly adores his girlfriend, Steph. Unfortunately, he also thinks she has a few physical imperfections, and when he mentions them, all hell breaks loose. "Tight, tense and emotionally true." *–Time Magazine.* "Lively and compulsively watchable." *–The Record.* [2M, 2W] ISBN: 978-0-8222-2394-8

★ **OPUS by Michael Hollinger.** With only a few days to rehearse a grueling Beethoven masterpiece, a world-class string quartet struggles to prepare their highest-profile performance ever—a televised ceremony at the White House. "Intimate, intense and profoundly moving." *–Time Out.* "Worthy of scores of bravissimos." *–BroadwayWorld.com.* [4M, 1W] ISBN: 978-0-8222-2363-4

★ **BECKY SHAW by Gina Gionfriddo.** When an evening calculated to bring happiness takes a dark turn, crisis and comedy ensue in this wickedly funny play that asks what we owe the people we love and the strangers who land on our doorstep. "As engrossing as it is ferociously funny." *–NY Times.* "Gionfriddo is some kind of genius." *–Variety.* [2M, 3W] ISBN: 978-0-8222-2402-0

★ **KICKING A DEAD HORSE by Sam Shepard.** Hobart Struther's horse has just dropped dead. In an eighty-minute monologue, he discusses what path brought him here in the first place, the fate of his marriage, his career, politics and eventually the nature of the universe. "Deeply instinctual and intuitive." *–NY Times.* "The brilliance is in the infinite reverberations Shepard extracts from his simple metaphor." *–TheaterMania.* [1M, 1W] ISBN: 978-0-8222-2336-8

DRAMATISTS PLAY SERVICE, INC.
440 Park Avenue South, New York, NY 10016 212-683-8960 Fax 212-213-1539
postmaster@dramatists.com www.dramatists.com

NEW PLAYS

★ **AUGUST: OSAGE COUNTY by Tracy Letts.** WINNER OF THE 2008 PULITZER PRIZE AND TONY AWARD. When the large Weston family reunites after Dad disappears, their Oklahoma homestead explodes in a maelstrom of repressed truths and unsettling secrets. "Fiercely funny and bitingly sad." –*NY Times.* "Ferociously entertaining." –*Variety.* "A hugely ambitious, highly combustible saga." –*NY Daily News.* [6M, 7W] ISBN: 978-0-8222-2300-9

★ **RUINED by Lynn Nottage.** WINNER OF THE 2009 PULITZER PRIZE. Set in a small mining town in Democratic Republic of Congo, RUINED is a haunting, probing work about the resilience of the human spirit during times of war. "A full-immersion drama of shocking complexity and moral ambiguity." –*Variety.* "Sincere, passionate, courageous." –*Chicago Tribune.* [8M, 4W] ISBN: 978-0-8222-2390-0

★ **GOD OF CARNAGE by Yasmina Reza, translated by Christopher Hampton.** WINNER OF THE 2009 TONY AWARD. A playground altercation between boys brings together their Brooklyn parents, leaving the couples in tatters as the rum flows and tensions explode. "Satisfyingly primitive entertainment." –*NY Times.* "Elegant, acerbic, entertainingly fueled on pure bile." –*Variety.* [2M, 2W] ISBN: 978-0-8222-2399-3

★ **THE SEAFARER by Conor McPherson.** Sharky has returned to Dublin to look after his irascible, aging brother. Old drinking buddies Ivan and Nicky are holed up at the house too, hoping to play some cards. But with the arrival of a stranger from the distant past, the stakes are raised ever higher. "Dark and enthralling Christmas fable." –*NY Times.* "A timeless classic." –*Hollywood Reporter.* [5M] ISBN: 978-0-8222-2284-2

★ **THE NEW CENTURY by Paul Rudnick.** When the playwright is Paul Rudnick, expectations are geared for a play both hilarious and smart, and this provocative and outrageous comedy is no exception. "The one-liners fly like rockets." –*NY Times.* "The funniest playwright around." –*Journal News.* [2M, 3W] ISBN: 978-0-8222-2315-3

★ **SHIPWRECKED! AN ENTERTAINMENT—THE AMAZING ADVENTURES OF LOUIS DE ROUGEMONT (AS TOLD BY HIMSELF) by Donald Margulies.** The amazing story of bravery, survival and celebrity that left nineteenth-century England spellbound. Dare to be whisked away. "A deft, literate narrative." –*LA Times.* "Springs to life like a theatrical pop-up book." –*NY Times.* [2M, 1W] ISBN: 978-0-8222-2341-2

DRAMATISTS PLAY SERVICE, INC.
440 Park Avenue South, New York, NY 10016 212-683-8960 Fax 212-213-1539
postmaster@dramatists.com www.dramatists.com